PREGNANT MISTRESSES

She's having his baby—
but she longs for his love...

She's been seduced in the bedroom, and now
she's pregnant by the man of her dreams.
But will she ever have the one thing she wants
more than anything—his ⬚⬚⬚

Don't miss any of ⬚⬚⬚⬚⬚⬚⬚⬚⬚⬚ in

Al⬚⬚⬚ ⬚⬚ ⬚he Boss
Natalie Anderson

Bedded by a Playboy
Heidi Rice

The Pregnancy Ultimatum
Kate Hardy

Married in a Rush
Julie Cohen

The Italian's Pregnancy Proposal
Maggie Cox

KATE HARDY lives on the outskirts of Norwich with her husband, two small children, a dog—and too many books to count! She wrote her first book at age six, when her parents gave her a typewriter for her birthday, and she had the first of a series of sexy romances published at twenty-five. She swapped a job in marketing communications for freelance health journalism when her son was born, so she could spend more time with him. She's wanted to write for Harlequin since she was twelve.

Kate is always delighted to hear from readers. Do drop in to her Web site at www.katehardy.com.

Kate Hardy

The Pregnancy Ultimatum

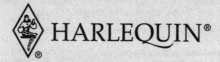

HARLEQUIN®

TORONTO • NEW YORK • LONDON
AMSTERDAM • PARIS • SYDNEY • HAMBURG
STOCKHOLM • ATHENS • TOKYO • MILAN • MADRID
PRAGUE • WARSAW • BUDAPEST • AUCKLAND

ISBN-13: 978-0-373-82088-7
ISBN-10: 0-373-82088-7

THE PREGNANCY ULTIMATUM

First North American Publication 2008.

Previously published in the U.K. under the title
IN THE GARDENER'S BED.

The Pregnancy Ultimatum

For Julie C and Diane, with love—
and thanks for the techie help...

CHAPTER ONE

So MUCH for the paperless office, Amanda thought as she hefted the two enormous briefcases off the tube. But this was probably giving her arms as much of a workout as she'd have got at the gym. And she didn't have time for the gym tonight anyway; if she wanted to get these schedules signed off, she needed to get home, grab a ready meal from the freezer, and eat it while she worked on the files.

The moment she walked in to the flat and sniffed the air, she knew she didn't stand much chance. Dee was clearly entertaining this evening. And her flatmate's friends, being an arty lot, were *loud*. With the amount of red wine that was bound to be consumed tonight, she'd need to add another item to her mental to-do list: *insert earplugs*.

'Hey, Mand! I was beginning to wonder if you were planning to sleep at the office tonight,' Dee teased, coming out of the kitchen.

'No.' Though perhaps she should've done—at least then she could've avoided having to be nice to people she knew didn't really like her. Dee was a sweetheart, but Amanda knew only too well that she didn't fit in with the rest of Dee's crowd. She was too quiet, too serious, not someone who made the room sparkle with her witty conversation. 'Sorry, I didn't realise you had people round tonight.' She gave Dee an apologetic smile. 'Let me nuke something in the microwave and I'll be out of your way in less than ten minutes.'

'No, no and no,' Dee said.

Amanda frowned. 'What?'

'No, I don't have anyone coming round. No, you're not eating your usual rubbish—you're having a decent meal, for once. And, no, you're not holing up in your room all evening with a pile of work.' Dee ticked the points off on her fingers. 'Especially not on a Friday night.'

Amanda stared at her flatmate. 'You've cooked for me?' They'd agreed the ground rules ages ago: they shared all the chores except cooking. Half the time Amanda ate out, and she was a hopeless cook, so she didn't think it fair to subject her flatmate to burnt offerings.

Then she had a nasty thought. 'Dee, is this your way of telling me that you're going to move out with Josh and I'm going to need a new flatmate?'

'Don't be so paranoid!' Dee smiled. 'It's nothing.'

It didn't feel like 'nothing'. It didn't look like it, either, from the expression on Dee's face.

'I just thought you deserved a treat. You've had a rubbish couple of weeks and you work too hard,' Dee said.

That was a sore point. Amanda was still stinging from last week's appraisal, and right now she could do without the work–life balance lecture she normally got from Dee.

'So I'm cooking you dinner tonight to give you a break. A girly chat'll do you good.'

Amanda wasn't so sure about that. She'd never been much good at girly chats. Numbers and percentages were so much easier to deal with than people were.

'I've made us Cajun chicken with sweet potato mash, green beans and roasted peppers,' Dee tempted.

It sounded almost as good as it smelled, and Amanda knew from experience that it would taste even better—Dee's cooking was legendary.

'Oh, and panna cotta with raspberries. Home-made.'

Pudding to die for—Amanda's big weakness. 'OK, I'm sold,' she said with a smile. 'But you've gone to a lot of trouble, Dee. It hasn't made you late with a deadline or anything, has it?'

'No-o.'

Was it her imagination, or did Dee sound slightly guilty?

She found out, the second after she'd taken the first delectable bite.

'I, um, need a favour,' Dee said, wriggling on her seat. 'The thing is, you know I want to work in TV, produce programmes?'

Amanda nodded.

'You know my friend is a PA to a TV producer—well, she talked to her boss about one of my ideas. He says if I can give him some kind of pilot tape to back up my treatment, he might be able to get me a break of some sort.'

'That's brilliant news.' Though Amanda still didn't see why Dee needed her to do a favour. 'So what's it all about?'

Dee filled their wine glasses. 'I'm pitching a series called *Lifeswap*. About two people with opposite lifestyles spending a week with each other and learning from each other's lives.'

Reality TV. Just the kind of thing Amanda loathed. 'Sounds interesting,' she said politely, not wanting to hurt her friend.

'And you'd be perfect for the pilot.'

'Me?' Amanda frowned. 'How do you make that out?'

'City girl, works hard in high finance, never gets time to smell the roses.' Dee spread her hands. 'You're an extreme case.'

'Case?' She wasn't anyone's case, thank you very much!

Dee ignored Amanda's indignation. 'You'd be great to pair with someone else who does actually take time to smell the roses.'

'I don't *need* to smell the roses.' Amanda folded her arms. So this was the favour—Dee wanted her to be in the pilot. Swap lives with someone who was her complete opposite. 'You can't seriously want me to swap places with someone who spends all day in a beauty salon or messing about on a games console.'

Dee laughed. 'You'd go bananas in seconds! No, it's sort of…' She frowned, as if thinking about the best way to put it. 'Think of it as job enrichment. What different businesses can learn from each other.'

'It's a great idea, Dee—for someone else,' Amanda said. 'I don't need job enrichment. I'm perfectly happy as I am.'

'No, you're not. It's been over a week since your appraisal and you're still brooding about it.'

'Of course I'm not,' Amanda lied.

'You said your boss told you they want you to be more flexible. Doing this pilot would prove just how flexible you are,' Dee said, 'because you'll be able to show that you can do someone else's job for a week. A job in a totally different area than yours. Which means you can bring your skills to it to improve the other person's life, and learn some new ones that you can take back to your job and wave in your boss's face.'

'Maybe.' Right now, Amanda wasn't sure anything would convince her boss. Her face didn't fit—it was as simple as that.

'I think this'd work really well. You're photogenic, you have a clear voice with no obvious accent, and you're a complete professional at everything you do. That's why I'm asking you.'

'Flannelling me, more like.' Amanda laughed wryly. 'I'm no supermodel. And I've never done any acting in my life. I wouldn't know where to start.'

'This isn't acting. It's reality TV, so all you have to do is be yourself,' Dee reminded her. 'This could be good for both of us, Mand. You get to showcase your talents and prove to your boss that you're ready for promotion to the next level. And I make a superb pilot and get my chance to prove I can do the job. We both win. You're doing me a favour, yes—but you'd get something back from it, too.' She gave Amanda a mischievous smile. 'And I could make sure that whoever you swap lives with is a great cook and would make you panna cotta or some kind of lemony pudding every single day.'

Amanda raised an eyebrow. 'If I want panna cotta, I can buy it at the deli on the way home.'

'The deli's normally shut by the time *you* leave work,' Dee pointed out. 'And this would be home-made.'

Home-made food…And Dee had been talking opposites. 'You're not thinking of making me be a chef for a week, are you?' Amanda asked, horrified at the idea of being stuck in a hot kitchen with some temperamental chef who'd rant and rave at her.

Dee chuckled. 'I don't think anyone could teach you to cook in a *year*, let alone a week!'

'And I don't want to learn, either. Food's just fuel.' Amanda made a dismissive gesture with her hand. 'I'm not wasting time in the kitchen—'

'That you could spend working,' Dee said, rolling her eyes. 'Yeah, yeah. I've heard that a million times and I still don't agree with you.'

'So we agree to disagree.' Amanda leaned back in her chair. 'Have you got someone in mind?'

'I'm working on him. *It*,' Dee corrected herself swiftly.

'Him?' Amanda felt her eyes narrowing. Oh, no. 'This isn't some elaborate set-up for a blind date, is it?'

'No, no, no.' Dee crossed her splayed hands rapidly in the air. 'I'm not fixing you up with anyone.'

Ha. That made a change. 'Good. Because I'm perfectly happy being single. If I want to be the youngest partner ever in the firm, I don't have time for distractions,' Amanda reminded her flatmate. Especially as it seemed she was going to have to work twice as hard to prove herself worthy; it still rankled that the bloke in the office who'd failed his exams when she'd got distinctions had been promoted ahead of her. His face fitted, but she had to work twice as hard to make up for the fact that hers didn't.

'I was just thinking about you swapping lives with a bloke— showing the difference between the sexes, that sort of thing.'

'And he's going to be my complete opposite.'

'*Relax.* You just have different lifestyles.'

It sounded as if Dee really did have someone in mind. 'What does he do?'

'Not finance.' Dee sighed. 'Look, I know you're an *über*-planner, and it's probably driving you mad that I'm not giving you the full details, but until I've got both of you to agree to do the pilot I can't give you a proper brief.'

Both of you. So it was definitely someone Dee knew. One of her arty mates, then. 'Musician? Painter? Photographer?' Amanda guessed.

'I'll tell you as soon as I can. Just trust me on this,' Dee said firmly. 'Think of it as an opportunity to be flexible.'

Back to her appraisal again. 'Hmm. How long are we talking about, exactly?'

'Two weeks. You shadow this person for a week, and the person shadows you. You film some of the things that happen and talk to the camera about what you've learned from each other.'

'If I do it—and I mean *if*—I'd have to clear the shadowing side with my boss. And there'd have to be something built in about client confidentiality,' Amanda said thoughtfully. 'I'd probably need to take some leave to do my side of the shadowing.'

'You've got loads of time in lieu stacked up that you never take—and you didn't take all your holiday entitlement last year,'

Dee pointed out. 'They owe you. Mand, it'll be fun. Trust me. All you have to do is keep a video diary for a week and analyse the situation at the end, work out which bits of your life would make the other person's better and which bits of theirs would be good for you. What have you got to lose?'

Amanda didn't have an answer for that. She ate another spoonful of panna cotta and thought about it. 'I'll talk to my boss on Monday. If it's okay with work, I'll do it.'

'You,' Dee said, 'are a complete star.'

'And how's my best brother?' Fliss asked as she opened the front door.

'Your only brother,' Will corrected with a smile. 'And usually you insist on calling me your baby brother.' Though nowadays he was more likely to look after Fliss than the other way round.

'You're still my best brother.' Fliss hugged him. 'Thanks for coming round. I know your schedule's a bit mad right now.'

He ruffled her hair. 'That's this time of year for you. A never-ending round of sowing, potting, weeding…'

'And you love every second of it. Watching new life spring forth, caring for your plants, working a little magic in people's lives to change the space they hated into the space they'd always dreamed of.'

He grinned. 'You've finally learned my spiel, then.'

'Not spiel. It's how you are.' She smiled back. 'I appreciate it that you've shoehorned me in.'

'Hey. I've always got time for you. You know that.' Family was important. It was just a pity that their parents didn't feel the same way. He pushed the thought aside. 'So, what was so desperately important that you needed to see me rather than talk over the phone?'

'Come and sit down.' Fliss led the way into her kitchen, where the pile of exercise books told Will he'd found his sister halfway through marking her class's homework, and switched the kettle on.

'There isn't anything wrong with the baby?' Sudden fear for his sister clenched in his gut.

'No.' She smiled at him. 'Nothing like that. And Cal and I still want you to be godfather. I just need a bit of a favour, that's all. And I thought it'd be easier to explain face to face than over the phone.'

'What sort of favour?' Will asked, shepherding her into a chair and taking over the tea-making. 'Something to do with the school's sensory garden?' He'd helped them plan a workable layout, earlier in the spring—plants with textures and scent and colour. 'If you want me to come and do another session on the lifecycle of plants and plant some sunflower seeds with the kids, give me a list of dates and I'll fit one of them in for you.'

'No-o. The favour's not exactly for me.'

He frowned. 'Who, then?'

'Dee.'

'She's doing some article about gardening and health and wants some quotes? Sure.' He'd given Dee 'expert' comments before now. 'Tell her to email me with what she wants and the deadline.'

'It's a bit more complicated than that.'

He brought two mugs of tea over to the kitchen table and set one in front of her. 'Hit me with it, then, sis.'

'She needs you to swap lives with someone.'

'She what?'

Fliss pulled a face. 'Stop looking at me as if I've got two heads.'

'Strictly speaking, you have,' Will said, gesturing to her bump.

She flapped a hand at him. 'Be serious, for once. This is important. It's my best friend's big chance to break into TV. If Dee can put together a pilot of her idea, she's found someone who might be interested.' Fliss looked animated. 'The idea is, two people with opposite lifestyles swap over for a week and see what they can learn from each other.'

'So you want me to leave my clients in the hands of someone who doesn't even know how or when to water a plant, let alone understand soil types or putting the right plant in the right aspect?' Will shook his head. 'Sorry, Fliss. I like Dee a lot—but I'm not putting my business on the line for her.' He'd spent too long building it up.

'She's not going to take over from you—just shadow you for a week. Do what you do, under your direction,' Fliss explained.

'*She?*' His eyes narrowed.

'Well, you need to be opposites—that's why it's going to be called *Lifeswap*. You'll be perfect: country boy and city chick.'

Will laughed. 'Small problem. Last time I looked, I lived in a city.' Though his laughter was hollow. City chick? No, thanks. He'd spent too many years of his life already with a woman who was so wedded to her career, she'd stuck her children into boarding school at the first opportunity—and palmed them off on to any relative who'd have them in the holidays. Thank God for Martin, their father's elder brother.

'We could get round that for the film, if you stayed at Martin and Helen's holiday cottage in the middle of the Fens and did some work for the garden centre. It'd be good publicity for you.'

He reached out and ruffled his sister's hair. 'Fliss, it's sweet of you to think of me, but I'm doing fine. I don't need publicity. I've got a six-month waiting list of people wanting me to give their gardens a makeover. And, yes, I know I could expand the business and take on some staff, but I like being hands on. I like seeing my clients personally—I like being the one who gives them that corner of magic in their life.'

'You're a control freak,' Fliss grumbled.

'No, I'm not. But people come to me because they want *me* to design their garden. It wouldn't be fair to palm them off on someone else. And if I expand, I'll spend half my life shuffling paperwork and the only plants I'll see will be stuck in pots in my office. Stuck in one place, like me.' He grimaced. 'No, thanks.'

Fliss took a sip of tea. 'See. You're opposites. She's wedded to her office. You're wedded to the outdoors.'

Wedded. He didn't like the sound of that word. Or the gleam in his sister's eye. 'Fliss, this isn't one of your hare-brained schemes to set me up with someone, is it?' His sister, being happily married and pregnant, wanted him to feel just as settled and was for ever introducing him to potential Misses Right. It drove him crazy because she refused to see that, right now, his career took up all his time. 'Because if it is, let me tell you yet *again* that I'm not ready to settle down with anyone. If and when I decide that I am, I'm quite capable of choosing Miss Right for myself.'

Fliss gave him a wicked grin. 'The last six have been…um…'

'*Not* Miss Right. Which I knew when I dated them. It was for fun, not for ever, and they knew from the start I wasn't planning to settle down with them.' He coughed. 'And if you're going to mention Nina, don't. Even you didn't see that one coming—and my solicitor's letter sorted it out.'

'But you haven't dated anyone since. You've let her get to you and ruin your life.'

Will laughed. 'Stop fussing. My life isn't ruined at all. I just haven't met anyone lately who interests me enough to want to date them. And if this is your idea of setting me up with someone, then you'll just have to explain to her that you made a mistake, because your little brother is a grown-up who knows his own mind.'

'Point taken. And this isn't a set-up—this really is for Dee's pilot programme.' Fliss sighed. 'Look, if you don't want to do it for your business, you could do it for Martin's. You know he's struggling to compete with the garden-centre chains.'

'I put as much business as I can his way,' Will reminded her. 'My clients like the unusual plants he grows.'

But it wasn't enough, and they both knew it.

'Publicity like this would be good for him,' Fliss said gently.

'Yes. And I know how much I owe him,' Will said, equally softly. 'Not just for all the school holidays when the parents dumped us on him. He's taught me so much about plants. And he backed me all the way when I decided to study horticulture—even gave me somewhere to live.' Not that their parents had actually thrown Will out. He just hadn't been able to live with the constant comments about how there was no money in gardening and the City was crying out for high flyers—people who were expected to get straight As at A-level and had been offered an unconditional place at Oxford. 'And he recommended me to customers at the garden centre when I started up on my own. Doing this would be—well—my chance to pay some of that back.'

'Your decision, bro.' Fliss held up her hands. 'As you said, you're a big boy now. And you have the right to say no.'

He smiled at her. 'I'm glad you realise that. But okay, I'll do it. Assuming the holiday cottage is available.'

'I've already checked. It's available in a fortnight's time.'

'And if Martin's happy for me to do this,' he warned. 'You might be interfering in his plans.'

Fliss grinned. 'No, I'm not. And of course he'll say yes to his favourite nephew. Not to mention the fact that it's a brilliant excuse for Helen to make him take a week's holiday.'

Will ignored her. 'And *if*,' he emphasised, 'my clients give permission.'

She smiled. 'Nobody ever says no to you, Will.'

Not quite true. The two people he'd always wanted to say 'yes' had usually said 'not now'…but there never *had* been a time for 'now'. He looked at his sister, unsmiling for once. 'So, what do you know about this woman I'm supposed to be swapping lives with?'

'Lives in London. Accountant. Knows nothing about plants.' Fliss ticked off the points on her fingers.

Accountant? Ouch. Still, it could've been worse—it could've been banking. Though something in his sister's expression tipped him off. 'Do you actually know her, Fliss?'

She winced. 'Sort of.'

'And?'

'Let's just leave it that she's your opposite, Will.'

He shook his head. 'I've got a bad feeling about this. Look, I can ask around and see if anyone else could help Dee.'

'But then Martin would lose out,' Fliss put in quietly. 'Which isn't fair.'

Will stared at her. 'That's manipulative, Fliss. Worthy of our mother.' That was the biggest insult he could throw at her.

Fliss ignored the barb. 'Dee's desperate to get this right, Will. She needs a real flora-and-fauna guy, someone who knows birdsong and wildlife and the countryside.'

He sighed. 'I'm an *urban* landscape gardener. My clients all live in a city. So do I.'

'But you know about birdsong and wildlife and the countryside. Look, you got the highest mark in the history of your degree course. You know exactly what you're doing.' Fliss rolled her eyes. 'And you'd be perfect on screen.'

'I'm not looking to be a TV gardener,' he warned.

'It might,' Fliss pointed out, 'force our dear parents into acknowledging what you do for a living. They might even admit that you're a raging success and you made the right choice in turning down that place at Oxford.'

He shrugged. 'I don't need their approbation. I already know I made the right choice.'

'And you're fast becoming one of the best-respected names in the business,' Fliss said. 'But look at you. Tall, dark and hand-some—and I'm not just biased because I'm your big sister. You'd look great on the pilot, you're laid back and unflappable, and you've got a lovely voice.'

'So, if this woman's my opposite, from your description, that'd make her short, blonde, ugly, uptight and with a voice like a foghorn?' he asked.

'She's short, blonde and pretty, actually,' Fliss corrected. 'But you're warm. She's ice. You connect with people. She's in an ivory tower.'

'And I'm meant to learn something from her?' Will asked with a raised eyebrow. 'Like what?'

'Well, you're a bit too soft-hearted and—oh!' She clapped a hand over her mouth.

He laughed. 'Maybe I should start toughening up right now, then. By saying no,' he teased.

'Please, Will. Dee deserves this chance. And it'll do Martin some good, too.'

He sighed. 'All right. I'll look at my schedule, see what I can rearrange, and sweet-talk my clients. But I'm doing this for Martin. And if this woman turns out to be the woman from hell…'

'You'll be fine,' Fliss said. 'You're good with people.' She patted her bump. 'Bambino, it should go on record that you have the best uncle in the world.'

'Only because I had a good role model. Uncle-wise, anyway.' Their parents were role models for how *not* to bring up your kids, and he knew Fliss thought the same.

'You're a star.' Fliss smiled at him. 'Thanks. You won't regret it. And it's only for two weeks.'

'Fourteen days. Three hundred and thirty-six hours.' He grimaced. 'Twenty thousand—'

'Stop, stop, stop,' Fliss said, holding up both hands. 'I can't calculate that quickly in my head. Are you *sure* you're not a secret banker?'

'Very funny.' Not. No way in hell would he work in high finance.

He didn't *like* the people from that world. The way they appreciated the price of everything and the value of nothing. He tried for lightness. 'Don't let the parents hear you say that.'

But the bitterness must have sounded in his voice, because Fliss shook her head. 'Hey. They're way past pressuring you. You stood up to them over ten years ago and you did the right thing.'

'Yeah.' He sighed. Even if this woman turned out to be an utter pain, he'd make sure the pilot programme was good. For Martin's sake, and Fliss's. 'Give me Dee's number, then. I'll ring her and tell her I'll do it.'

CHAPTER TWO

THE MIDDLE of nowhere. That was the only way to describe where Will Daynes lived.

Amanda groaned inwardly as she parked outside the little cottage. If anything, this was worse than the village where she'd grown up. At least there *had* been a village, even if it had been a tiny place with a school, a pub and a post office-cum-village shop. Here, there was nothing round the cottage at all. Just the Fens, stretching out for miles and miles. Flat, featureless fields.

And this was where she was supposed to spend the next seven days. Shadowing a garden centre manager. Right now, she wasn't sure if she'd last seven hours in a place like this, let alone seven days! Some people thought the country was a place for lovely days out—pretty scenery and birds singing and what have you. Amanda knew better. The country meant being lonely—never fitting in, with nowhere to go and nothing to do. No wonder her mother had become so distant and bad tempered, being stuck there. The country was a *trap*.

Then she remembered. *Flexibility*. She wasn't going to give up before she'd even started. Though what on earth Dee thought she could possibly learn from a backwater like this…

She climbed out of the car, marched over to the front door and rang the bell.

No reply.

She frowned. She knew Will was expecting her. So why wasn't he here to meet her? Unless he'd had to deal with some sort of crisis at the garden centre—wherever that was—and hadn't been able to get in touch with her. Maybe he'd called Dee. Though surely Dee would've texted her to let her know he was going to be late?

She rang the doorbell again. Still no reply.

Impatiently, she grabbed her mobile phone. No texts. She punched the speed-dial number for home.

'Hel-lo.' Dee sounded distracted.

'Dee, it's Amanda.'

'Hello? Hello? Is anyone there?'

'It's *Amanda*!' she yelled.

'Oh, sorry! You sound really faint. Is everything all right?'

'No. Nobody's here.' And it made her want to stamp her foot in frustration. 'Have you heard anything from Will Daynes?'

'No. But don't worry. He knows you're coming. Unless you're early?'

'Ten minutes,' Amanda was forced to admit. Because she was never late for anything. Ever.

'That'll be it, then. Chill. He'll be there when he said he would be. Enjoy your week.'

Amanda wished she could be as sure as Dee sounded. But Will hadn't given her any of the kind of details she'd given him. He hadn't sent her a photograph or contact details, so she had no idea what he looked like or how to get in touch with him, except via Dee. He'd given her no idea about what she'd be expected to wear, or the sort of schedule they'd have for the week. And as for confidentiality agreements…

Well. At least he'd returned *her* agreement. Signed in a bold, spiky script. And he'd sent her a hastily scribbled set of directions to the cottage on a scrap of paper. Ha. If he'd given her the postcode of the cottage, she could've used SatNav. As it was, she'd had to rely on him. He hadn't even given her enough information for her to pinpoint the place on a map.

To be fair, his directions had been perfect. But it still niggled her that she'd given him a decent brief and he'd given her not the faintest clue. She hated being in a situation where she couldn't plan ahead. What kind of a man was Will Daynes, anyway?

But there was nothing she could do about it, and no point in wasting time. She opened the boot and fished out the little video camera Dee had lent her. 'Day one,' she said. 'I've arrived. Nobody's in. And I've never seen a place so empty. It's bleak in the summer, so I hate to think what it'd be like in the winter. I don't know about taking time to smell the roses—there *are* no roses, here. Just endless flat fields and huge skies.'

She panned a shot of the fenlands, to show the viewers what she meant. *Keep a video diary*, Dee had said. *Be honest. It doesn't matter if you use loads of tape; I'd rather have too much than too little, so I can edit everything down.* 'I don't think I'm going to learn anything from this lifeswap week. Other than that London's definitely the right place for me.' And that Will clearly didn't bother preparing and planning things. Not that she was going to be rude about him right now. She'd reserve judgement until she actually met him.

'This place is such a backwater,' she said, leaning against the car with her eyes closed, 'and I want to go home.'

'Given up before you've even started?' a quiet, slightly posh voice asked.

Amanda shrieked and nearly dropped the camera. Just in time, she rescued it and switched it off. 'Oh, my God! Where did *you* come from?' she demanded.

He pointed to the battered-looking estate car parked behind hers—the car she hadn't even heard pull up behind her—and gave her a faint smile. 'Amanda Neave, I presume.'

'Yes. And you must be William Daynes.'

'Will,' he corrected.

True to form, he was her complete opposite even in that, preferring the short form of his first name.

She took the time to study him, and then wished she hadn't when she felt a weird twinge in the region of her heart.

How corny was that?

But Will Daynes was a heartthrob. No wonder Dee had wanted him for her pilot. Female viewers would just melt at their first glimpse of him. Tall, with fair skin—very fair, considering he must spend a good deal of his time outdoors—and very dark hair. Curly—messy, even—and a bit too long; obviously the owner of the garden centre Will managed wasn't a stickler for appearances, then. Broad shoulders and a firm chest hugged by a black T-shirt, and long, long legs encased in denim so faded and soft it made her want to reach out and touch. She only just stifled the impulse.

And then there were his eyes.

They were most stunning light green colour; no, on second thoughts, they weren't so much green as gold. Grey. Silvery. A strange, unearthly mixture of colours. Incredible. Beautiful.

Or maybe these wide-open spaces were getting to her.

'And this is Sunny.' A brown-and-white springer spaniel sat at his heels, eyeing Amanda curiously, but clearly having no intention of moving without her master's permission.

Dee hadn't said anything about a dog.

Amanda had spent the last twenty-four years avoiding dogs. Oh, lord. Why hadn't Dee warned her? Or why hadn't she thought of it for herself? Of *course* a country boy would have a dog. More than one, perhaps.

How was she going to cope if he had three or four?

'Hello, Sunny.' Involuntarily, she took the tiniest step backwards.

And he clearly noticed, because he said quietly, 'She won't hurt you.'

What a first impression she'd made. He'd overheard what she'd said about this place. And now she'd flinched away from his dog. He'd have her pegged as a complete coward who ran away from things. Which wasn't how she was, at all.

'Just stretch your hand out and let her sniff you. She won't bite. Though she might lick you.' He ruffled the dog's fur. 'I think she'd probably lick a burglar to death—wouldn't you, girl? She's Sunny by name and sunny by nature.'

Gingerly, Amanda stretched out her hand. At a nod from Will, the dog stepped forward, sniffed Amanda's fingers and gave her an experimental lick that took all of Amanda's backbone not to snatch her hand away. And then the dog sat politely, thumped her tail against the ground once, and looked expectantly at Amanda.

'She's waiting for you to stroke the top of her head,' Will said.

Flexibility, Amanda reminded herself inwardly, and tried it.

'Oh! Her fur's really soft.' She'd expected something that felt rough and wiry, whereas Sunny's fur was more like that of an old-fashioned, well-loved teddy bear.

Sunny's tail thumped again; and Will was still wearing that enigmatic smile. Mona Lisa had nothing on him. Amanda hated the fact that she hadn't worked him out. She was good at judging people quickly. With Will Daynes, she didn't even know where to start.

'Come in,' he said. 'Where are your things?'

'I'll manage,' she said, lifting her chin.

'I'm sure you can,' he said drily, 'but I was brought up to look after my guests.'

And she was a guest. For a week. In his house. In his life.

Without another word, she opened the boot of her car. She let him take her single suitcase and followed him and the dog into the house.

He led her up the stairs. 'Your room,' he said, opening the door and setting her suitcase next to the bed. A double, she noticed.

'If you want to freshen up, the bathroom's there.' He indicated a door at the end of the corridor. 'There are a couple of fresh towels in your room; if you need any more, they're here, in the airing cupboard.'

The remaining door, she assumed, belonged to his room.

'I'll be in the kitchen when you're ready.' He gave her another of those faint smiles, and left.

Amanda blew out a breath and sat down on the bed. Home for the next week. Though this didn't really feel like a home. Everything was neutral. Pastel. There was a painting on the wall—a watercolour of a garden—but it, too, was neutral. Nothing like what she'd expected from a gardener's house.

Though what *had* she expected? Will had given her nothing to go on, and Dee had refused to give her much more information other than that he was a 'good sort'. Hmm. As his opposite, did that make her a 'bad sort'?

She pushed the thought away. She really needed to talk to Will and find out what was going to happen this week.

She unpacked her things swiftly, made a swift detour to the bathroom—another neat, neutral room—and splashed her face with water, then headed downstairs.

Kitchen, he'd said.

She followed her nose. Something smelled *gorgeous*.

Will was stirring something in a pan on the cooker. 'Lunch,' he said, pouring a bright green soup into two white bowls and setting them on the scrubbed pine table. 'Help yourself to bread and cheese.' There was a loaf sitting on a wooden board next to a bread-knife, a white shallow dish of butter, another white dish containing tomatoes and a plate with a large hunk of cheese.

Rustic. But more fuss than she'd have made; on Saturday she normally grabbed a slice of toast for lunch, if she bothered with anything at all.

'Thanks.' She gave him an awkward smile and slid into one of the chairs. At the first taste of the soup, she felt her eyes widen. 'This is lovely. Where did you buy it?'

He lifted an eyebrow. 'The mint's from my garden and the courgettes were from the farmer's market.'

It took a moment to sink in. 'You *made* this?'

He shrugged. 'Just before breakfast. So it's had time to let the flavours develop.'

Dee hadn't been joking, then, when she'd said she'd find Amanda someone who cooked.

'It's, um, very nice.' And what an idiot he must think her. 'Are the tomatoes from your garden, too?'

He shook his head. 'Farmers' market. Mine aren't quite ready yet.'

Right then, Amanda wished she'd boned up on gardening. Read a few books. *Why* hadn't she prepared properly? She'd never be this slack with a new client. She always read up on the company's background, and made sure she knew about their competitors and their aims and what have you, so she could have an informed discussion right from the start. With Will, she'd done nothing. And she was already regretting it. 'I, um, don't know a lot about gardening,' she muttered.

'Isn't that the whole point of this lifeswap thing?' he asked.

'I suppose so.' How was it that she was putting her foot deeper and deeper into her mouth? In the city, she never had this problem. She always had the answers. Never said stupid things. Out here...

Out here, she was beginning to think she was a different person.

Amanda Neave wasn't anything like Will had expected. Small, blonde and pretty, according to Fliss. And an ice maiden. Uptight. At first glance, Fliss was spot on—even Amanda's eyes were an icy shade of blue. And she was pristine down to the last detail. He'd just bet she'd never walked through a garden in bare feet or muddy wellies. Her shoes would always be perfectly polished, her clothes without a wrinkle, her hair groomed into that sleek bob, her nails manicured.

Ha. She was a typical city girl who, from her biography on the company website, seemed ambitious with a razor-sharp mind and a very definite goal. He'd been absolutely spot on, preparing himself to deal with someone like his mother. Though there was one surprising difference. His mother wouldn't have been nervous about a dog—she'd have seen Sunny as a nuisance who ought to be kept out of sight. At least Amanda hadn't told him to get rid of the dog. Yet.

He watched her through lowered lids. Amanda Neave also had the most beautiful mouth he'd ever seen. And it was just as well they were here in Martin's holiday cottage rather than in his own home. Because, although Will had two spare rooms, he could imagine carrying her up the stairs to his room. To his bed. The thought sent a ripple of desire down his spine.

Desire he had no intention of acting on. He was doing this as a favour to his family and Dee—Amanda Neave was definitely the wrong sort of person for him to get involved with. His opposite. Undomesticated, business-oriented, the sort who'd put her career before everything else. He knew her type. And he also knew a hell of a lot better than to get involved with her—the sort of woman who had a calculator instead of a heart.

He tried not to let his hostility show. Telling Amanda what he thought of her kind wouldn't exactly be good for Dee's pilot. 'Help yourself to bread and what have you. So, how do you know Dee, then?' he asked.

'She's my flatmate.'

That surprised him. Why would someone as laid back and relaxed as Dee share a flat with a control freak? Amanda was definitely a control freak: the dossier she'd sent him via Dee proved that. The business confidentiality thing he could appreciate, given her job—but the schedules and timetables she'd given him were rigid and inflexible. No way was he letting Amanda push him into providing the same sort of information for her. That wasn't how he worked. And this week, just to emphasise the differences between them for Dee's pilot, he'd push that lack of structure to its extreme.

'What about you?' she asked.

He shrugged. 'She's my sister's best friend.'

For a second, shock registered on her face. 'Fliss Harrison's your sister?'

'Mmm. She mentioned that she knew you.'

He'd never seen a face shutter so quickly. Fliss clearly hadn't liked Amanda much and it was entirely mutual, but Amanda was obviously too polite to say so—and didn't want to hear what Fliss had had to say about her, either.

'So, what are the plans for this week?'

He hid a smile. Her abrupt change of topic was a clear attempt to get things back under control. *Her* control. Well, this was his week. Which meant it wasn't going to be regimented—at all. In fact, he was going to push her right to her limits.

'Depends on the weather,' he drawled.

'On the weather?' There was a gratifying squeak in her voice before she got herself back under control. 'But I thought you were a garden centre manager?'

Uh-oh. He'd slipped up already. 'Sort of. I'm only at the centre for some of the time.' So far, so true. 'I have more of a specialist role.' It just happened to be for himself, not for Martin.

'Doing what?'

Best to stick to the whole truth, this time. 'I design gardens.'

'You mean decking and water features and what have you?'

She'd obviously caught some TV gardening programmes. He grimaced. 'Personally, I'm not into catwalk gardening.'

She frowned. 'Catwalk?'

'Fashionable stuff,' he explained. 'Fashions change. And that leaves my client stuck with something that maybe he doesn't really like. Designing a garden's more than just digging holes, plonking in a few shrubs and sculptures or what have you and hoping for the best.'

'Oh?'

There was the faintest tinge of disbelief in the word, and Will felt his hackles rise. She was definitely from his parents' world; she even had the same attitude as they did towards gardening. That it wasn't really a valid career—that it was something you only did if you weren't bright enough to go into finance or computing or law or medicine.

And it annoyed him intensely that she'd managed to get the same reaction from him that they did. Getting him on the defensive within seconds. He didn't *need* to defend himself. Not to her. And yet the words came out anyway, crisp and haughty, and he hated it the way he'd let her make him sound. 'On the kind of garden makeovers you see on TV, they use mature plants so there aren't any gaps to be filled. Mature plants are expensive. If you take the average person's budget, the plants they can afford will be a lot smaller, so it'll take time for the garden to grow into the design.'

'I see.'

No, she didn't. And he needed to make her understand. 'It depends on the kind of soil and the aspect of the space—that means the light and the shape of the area. And, most importantly, it depends on the client's lifestyle and how they want to use the space. A design only works if it fits the client's needs properly. It's part experience, part experiment and part instinct.'

She looked at him. 'So what sort of garden would you design for me?'

'I don't know you well enough to answer that properly.' He'd need to talk to her, fill in the mental questionnaire he went through when discussing a garden with a new client. 'But I'd hazard a guess that you'd prefer a low-maintenance garden with an automatic watering system that you don't have to think about. Something formal, maybe slightly minimalist, that wouldn't be disturbed by kids and pets.' He'd just bet that if her flat had a garden, Amanda never set foot in it, because she would always be at the office. 'And all the flowers would be white,' he added before he could stop himself. Cool and glacial. Just like Amanda herself.

She didn't seem to take offence. 'Are you seeing any clients this week?'

'Maybe.'

'Scared I might frighten them off?' She raised an eyebrow. 'That's why you didn't send me an agenda for the week.'

'Partly,' he admitted. He'd wanted to see what she was like, first.

'I'm always polite to clients. There's no point in being otherwise. And if you don't listen to what they want, you won't do a good job because you won't be meeting their needs.' She cut herself a piece of bread. 'Which is what you said about making a good design for a garden. Maybe we're not so far apart, after all.'

He raised an eyebrow. 'I doubt it. For a start, I don't organise my time down to the last second.'

'So you could be wasting time. Maybe that's what Dee thinks you'll learn from me. Organisation.'

Was she trying to rattle him? Lord, she sounded exactly like his parents. He'd just bet she did her filing several times a day. 'Who says I'm not organised?' He wasn't tidy, true, but he knew exactly where everything was. 'Besides, creative jobs need thinking time.'

'Planning time,' she corrected. 'And there's a point where you have to start acting on those plans, or you'll just drift and fall behind your schedule.'

She was wasted in the civilian world, he thought; with that efficiency and precision, she should've been something military. She'd make a great field marshal. Crisp and incisive.

Battling with her was probably going to be a mistake. But it was either that or… No, he couldn't possibly start liking her. She was meant to be his opposite. The sort he detested. That funny little feeling in his stomach…he'd probably just drunk too much coffee today. It wasn't desire. He couldn't want her.

'You're forgetting something. It's not possible to control the weather. If it's blowing a gale, you don't sow seeds outdoors.'

'I might not know a lot about gardening, but even *I* know you wouldn't plant seeds outside in the middle of winter.'

Was that the hint of a smile? No. She was absolutely serious. Too serious. Though he couldn't help wondering what Amanda would look like if she smiled. Ha. It was probably a good idea that he didn't find out. Because that beautiful mouth, once curved, might be impossible to resist. Okay, he might despise her world and everything she stood for, but he couldn't stay in denial for ever. The physical attraction was there.

He also couldn't deny that lust wasn't a decent basis for a relationship. He could never, ever, have a relationship with a woman like Amanda Neave—someone who didn't understand his world, didn't want to understand his world and would expect him to give up his dreams for a 'proper' job. 'Winter's not the only time when it's blowy. March is a good time to sow outdoors. Think of March winds and April showers,' he said.

'Then you have contingency plans.'

'Does everything have to be planned?' he asked. 'The best gardens start out as an experiment. They change. Adapt. It takes *years* to make the right garden for you. And even then it might not be the right garden a year later—your circumstances might have changed.'

'So you adapt the plan,' she said firmly.

'Are you ever spontaneous?' he asked. 'Or is everything rigidly fixed?'

For a second, he thought he saw her flinch. But she rallied. 'I can be flexible.'

He doubted it. But maybe that was what Dee thought she'd learn from him. The art of adapting.

Ha. Who were they trying to kid? Amanda wouldn't adapt. She'd expect his world to adapt to her, instead. This lifeswap thing was going to be a nightmare.

Especially because his heart was trying to overrule his head, to drop in sneaky suggestions. Like wondering how soft her mouth was. Or whether those ice-blue eyes would go all soft and dreamy when she'd just been kissed. And—

No. Absolutely no. He wasn't going to fantasise about Amanda Neave. He'd get through the next thirteen and a half days, and everything would be fine.

CHAPTER THREE

'YOU COOKED lunch. Washing up's the least I can do.' It was the deal Amanda had with Dee, on the rare occasions they ate together. Trading skills. And Amanda hated to be beholden to anyone in any way.

Will shook his head. 'Guests don't wash up. Sit down and finish your coffee.'

'I've finished my coffee.' She took a deep breath. 'And I'm not a guest, strictly speaking. I'm your shadow.'

'So you're intending to share the cooking with me tonight, then?'

Not in a million years. 'We could eat out,' she offered.

'We're meant to be opposites.' His eyes crinkled at the corners as he clearly realised the implications. 'You can't cook, can you?'

'I don't *need* to cook,' she said, aiming for loftiness.

He leaned against the sink, tipping his head on one side. 'No? Let me see. No cooking. So either you're one of these people who believe in eating only raw foods—in which case you would've refused to eat the soup at lunchtime—or you live on takeaways.'

'Neither.' She could feel herself blushing, and willed herself to remain cool about this. There was nothing wrong with choosing not to cook, was there? Not everyone needed to be into this domestic bliss stuff. 'Supermarkets sell perfectly adequate cook-chill food.'

He snorted. 'Do they, hell. I don't know what they do to white sauce, but it turns slimy, and the rest of it doesn't taste much better.' He paused. 'So are you telling me you see food as fuel, and nothing else?'

She shrugged. 'What else is it?'

She wished she hadn't asked when he drawled, 'Pleasure.'

Oh, lord. The pictures that word conjured up. Pictures involving his hands stroking her skin. His mouth skimming the hollows of her throat. His body sliding over hers, bare skin against bare skin, teasing her until—

No. She grabbed the tea-towel and snapped, 'Don't you think we should get the washing up out of the way?'

'Do we have a time limit? Interesting. How many seconds per plate, do you think?'

He was laughing at her, the rat. She really, really wanted to throw something at him.

Except he'd probably throw something back. The nearest thing was that bowl of sudsy water. Which would turn her white blouse completely transparent and…

What on earth was wrong with her? Since when did she start having sexy fantasies about men she barely knew? She didn't have *time* for this sort of thing. Hadn't her mother always drilled it into her? *Don't let sex get in the way of your career.* No matter how attractive a man was, he wasn't worth losing her place in the line for promotion.

She lifted her chin, ignoring his comment. 'I was rather hoping that you'd give me a tour of the garden centre this afternoon—if you weren't planning to do any other work I could shadow, that is. And as it's two o'clock already, we really should be getting a move on.'

Bossy didn't even begin to describe this woman. And Will had never met anyone so driven by time. He was very, very tempted to remove all the clocks in the house—including commandeering her watch and her mobile phone and stowing them in a safe place—to see how she reacted. To see if he could get her to slow down and take time to see that there was more to life than being stuck in an office.

But he said nothing. He simply washed up and allowed her to dry the crockery and cutlery. Meticulously, of course. Then he put the things away.

'I'll drive you over to the garden centre, then,' he said, settling Sunny in her basket. 'And you can look after the house for us, honey.' He fondled the dog's ears. 'No chewing, okay?' He didn't think she would—but at three years old, Sunny still had enough puppy left in her to do something mischievous from time to time. And this was the first time they'd stayed in the cottage. Please, don't let her do something mad like chewing a chair, Will thought; the house needed to be spick and span by eleven o'clock next Saturday morning for the new lot of guests.

'I really thought you'd be working today. I mean, aren't Saturdays and Sundays the busiest days at garden centres?' Amanda asked.

'With the weekend gardeners coming in for supplies, you mean? Uh-huh. Though we're not like the big chains, selling garden furniture and barbecues and the like. We're a specialist nursery.'

'Specialist?'

'We couldn't compete with the big chains in terms of price. So we differentiate ourselves by service and by providing a different product: old-fashioned English roses and apple trees, cottage garden plants—'

'That makes good business sense,' she said.

Was it really possible to want to push someone into a deep, muddy puddle and to kiss them senseless at the same time? 'I'm so glad you approve,' he said drily.

She flushed. 'I didn't mean to sound patronising. I'm sorry. I'm not very good at this.'

'Because you're used to being in an office. Driven by time.' He gave her a calculating look. 'Take off your watch.'

'What?'

'Take off your watch. Because it drives me crazy when you keep looking at it.'

Her flush deepened. 'I don't keep looking at my watch.'

'Maybe I should film you for five minutes, without you realising it, and make you watch the footage. Make you count for yourself how many times you check.'

For a moment, he thought she was going to make a smart comment; but she said nothing. Just took off her watch and stowed it in a compartment in her handbag. 'Anything else you'd like me to do?'

Kiss me.

He felt colour stain his own cheeks, then. What the hell was he thinking, letting his body rule his head? No way could anything happen between them. They were far too different.

Though all the same, he couldn't help wondering what her mouth would feel like beneath his. Or whether she'd kiss him back. Would the ice maiden melt and turn out to be warm and giving and—?

Hands off, he reminded himself. This is business. And he needed to prove to her that his business was just as important as hers.

'Hop in,' he said, ushering her to the car. He really, really hoped that the garden-centre staff would remember what he'd said in the team meeting this morning: while Martin was away, he was going to act as the manager for the week. He wouldn't be there all the time, and he'd have a shadow with him when he was in the office. If there were any problems while he was out at a client's, ring his mobile.

He wasn't expecting any major problems, though; most of the staff had worked with Martin since Will was a child, and the team gelled so well that the garden centre virtually ran itself. The admin side wouldn't do so well in Helen's absence—his aunt kept all the paperwork in order—but she'd taken pity on him and told him to leave anything that didn't need immediate attention.

The only thing that could go wrong was if someone forgot he was meant to be the manager and made some comment—because Amanda would pick up on it and ask questions. Just as well he was good at thinking on his feet.

For a moment, he was tempted to come clean and admit that he didn't live in the middle of nowhere and he hadn't worked at the garden centre since the year after he'd graduated. Whenever he did go to Daynes Nurseries, he spent his time choosing plants or sitting on the edge of his aunt's desk, eating her biscuits. But telling the truth would mean letting Dee down and letting his family down. He wasn't prepared to do that. When he made a promise, he kept it.

He climbed into the driver's side. 'One thing,' he said as he drove off, 'did you bring some more suitable clothes with you?'

'How do you mean?'

'Jeans, or something.'

'I always wear a suit to work.'

'For your job, that's fine. For mine, it's not practical. Do you actually *own* a pair of jeans, out of interest?'

Her face set. 'That's a personal question.'

'In other words, no.' He sighed. 'What did you think we'd do this week, sit in the office all day at the garden centre? You need clothes that can stand a bit of wear and tear. Something where it doesn't matter if you accidentally wipe mud on it. Something that won't crumple.'

He could hardly believe that she didn't own any jeans. And she was wearing a business suit today—on a Saturday, the weekend, when most people would wear something comfortable and casual. Was she always this buttoned up and formal?

Lord. She was going to find this week really tough. 'I can borrow some overalls from the garden centre for you,' he said, 'but… Oh, we'll sort that out later.'

Will lapsed into silence, and Amanda had plenty of time to study him. She noted that his hands were slightly rough, strong looking and yet fine at the same time. She also noted that his car was a complete mess—although her seat was clean, the back seat had a blanket on it covered in dog hair, and there was mud on the carpets as well as a pile of papers in the passenger footwell. For goodness' sake, hadn't he heard of a briefcase or even a cardboard folder to keep his papers together? Let alone a car vacuum cleaner…

Irritating, *irritating* man.

And it irritated her even more that her body wasn't agreeing. It was reacting to him. It wanted to move closer. Touch. Taste.

Absolutely not. She folded her arms to stop herself acting on temptation.

Ten minutes later, he turned into a gravelled driveway. She noticed the single-storey brick building bore a sign saying 'Daynes Nurseries'.

Then she remembered what he'd said earlier. 'I thought you were the manager here? Do you own it, too?' she asked.

'It's a family business,' he said, his face completely unreadable.

She followed him inside. There was a small area with a cash desk, but she couldn't see any of the gardening equipment, soft toys or plastic ornaments she'd expected to find in a garden centre. Just a coffee shop with watercolours lining the walls and a couple of display cases containing ceramics, a shelf with jars and a small notice about free-range eggs; the rest of the building appeared to lead to glasshouses.

He smiled and waved at the checkout staff, then shepherded her into an office. His, presumably—like his car, it was completely untidy with paperwork everywhere.

Odd, then, that his house was so neat.

There was more to Will Daynes than met the eye, she was sure, but she didn't have the chance to speculate further. 'There are some overalls in the bottom drawer,' he said. 'They should fit you—if they're a bit long, just roll the legs up a bit. You might as well change here.'

Change? What did he mean, change?

The question must have shown on her face because he said, 'Your suit's going to get a bit crumpled if you pull overalls on top of them.'

She hadn't thought of that. 'I…'

'Pull the blind. I'll get the overalls and stay outside the door until you're ready.' He gave her a sweet, sweet smile—a smile that told her he was enjoying her discomfiture—and closed the door behind him.

He thought she was going to chicken out? Ha. She'd show him. She pulled the blind, found the overalls, stripped off her suit, changed, rolled up the legs of the slightly-too-long overalls and was outside the door within a minute.

'Fast. Impressive.' He nodded, then glanced at her shoes. Her expensive, Italian designer shoes with kitten heels. 'They might get messy. What size shoe do you take?'

'Four.'

'We might have some wellies in your size. Otherwise you'll have to wear thick socks to make them fit.' He headed for a cupboard, rummaged inside. 'Ah. You're in luck.'

Green wellies, to go with her green overalls. She couldn't remember the last time she'd worn wellies, even as a child. Though at least these ones were new, still wrapped in a polythene bag. She really would've hated having to borrow someone else's boots.

'Right. Tour, first.'

Her cue to film, she thought.

He took her through to the greenhouse area and talked her

through the different groups of plants, telling her how they could be used to transform everything from a tiny patio to a huge formal garden. Amanda noticed how his eyes glittered with passion as he talked—the same passion she'd seen when he'd talked earlier about what designing a garden meant—and she could almost feel his enthusiasm sweeping her along.

Then he stooped down to show her a pale lilac flower that looked like a pastel-coloured gerbera. 'One of my favourites for borders,' he said.

The way his fingers gently caressed the petals made desire flicker down her spine. Would he touch her skin in the same way, treat her as if she were as delicate and rare and special? And the passion in his voice as he spoke about his plants—what would that passion be like, directed at a person rather than a plant? Directed at *her*?

Oh, lord. She couldn't start thinking like that about him. 'What is it?' she asked, hoping the heat she felt in her cheeks didn't actually show.

'*Dimorphotheca*—the rain daisy. You can use it as a weather forecaster. If it's open, it's going to be sunny all day. As soon as it closes, you'll know to bring the washing in.'

A functional plant. She liked the sound of that. And it was quite pretty, with its pale petals and strikingly dark middle.

Another wave from another green-overalled member of staff, which Will returned warmly. Hmm. Everyone here seemed pleased to see him; somehow Will Daynes made people smile. Something she wasn't aware of in her own job, probably because people were more focused on business.

She'd always thought that a good thing. Now, she wasn't so sure. Why didn't people smile around her like that? She was good at her job and what she did stopped people from worrying. So why didn't they relax around her, the way they seemed to relax around Will? Why did she still have that same awkward feeling she'd had as a child—the feeling of never quite fitting in?

To distract herself, she asked, 'You really love your job, don't you?'

'Life's too short not to. I couldn't be anything else but a gardener.'

It felt like an obscure comment on her own lifestyle. There was nothing wrong with what she did. A muscle tightened in her jaw and she switched off the camera. 'I love my job, too. I like being able to take the worry from my clients, by making everything neat and tidy for them.'

'Uh-huh.' He was clearly doing his best to sound neutral, but she had the sneaking suspicion that she'd amused him. Probably the words 'neat and tidy'. Well, not everyone wanted to live in chaos.

'Um…excuse me?' A nervous-looking woman stood next to them. 'Sorry to interrupt, but I was wondering if you could help me when you've finished with your customer?'

Amanda suddenly realised the woman was asking *her*, not Will. Because of the green overalls, no doubt. 'I'm afraid I don't actually know much about plants, but I can find someone for you.' She looked at Will, hoping he'd direct the customer to the right place.

'I'm Will Daynes,' he said with a smile, offering his hand. 'Amanda's actually an office specialist, working with me on a project. But I can help with plants, if you like.'

The woman shifted from foot to foot. 'I've just moved—it's my first house and my first garden, and I don't even know where to start. All I do know is I just don't want this horrible, bare concrete square.'

Will's smile broadened. 'Actually, that's the best sort of starting point because if there's nothing there it means you can have exactly what *you* want. Tell me more about it.'

Amanda watched in amazement as Will chatted to the woman, drawing her out and making her feel so at home that she stopped shifting from foot to foot and talked to him about her dream garden. He didn't make a single note, but clearly took in every detail she told him, because he then took a small notepad from the back pocket of his jeans and drew a quick map.

Then Amanda realised there had been a structure to the conversation. He'd found out the area's aspect, how much the woman wanted to spend, what she wanted from the area and her favourite colours. And he was actually sketching a design as he talked to her—a design based around pots and troughs, shrubs and bedding plants and herbs.

She followed him as he took the woman into the glasshouses, and showed her the sorts of plants he'd talked about and which ones she needed to start with. Then he told her how she could add to the garden over time, but one key shrub, some geraniums and some herbs would brighten it up until she'd had a chance to think more about the kind of plants she liked the look of. Finally he wrote down some instructions for her about how to look after the plants—when to water them, how much, what kind of feed they should have and how often.

'Thank you so much,' the woman said with a smile when Will found her a trolley, loaded the plants onto it and handed her the design sketch. 'My neighbour said Daynes was a good place to come. That they have time for you here—they don't just rush you into buying stuff you don't have a clue how to look after.'

Will smiled back. 'It's what we've always believed in.'

'I really appreciate it,' she said.

Time. Amanda went to glance at her watch, then remembered it was in her handbag. No way was she going to let him catch her looking at it. But how much time had Will spent with the customer? Surely it wasn't cost-productive use of his time, as the garden centre manager?

As if he'd guessed what she was thinking, he said, 'Time's relative. We have a satisfied customer who'll go and tell her friends about us. And word of mouth's the most effective kind of advertising.'

'Mmm.'

'There's a big difference,' he said softly, 'between value and worth. I could cost out the price of my time—but you can't put a price on the happiness that woman's going to get from her garden. And *that*'s important. It's why she came here.'

Amanda nodded slowly.

'So what *is* the time?' he asked.

She knew that he was teasing her, and decided to call his bluff. 'No idea.'

'Actually, I meant it.' He took out his mobile phone and glanced at the screen. 'Right. That'll do here for today. There's something we need to do.'

'What?'

'Go shopping.'

'Shopping? What for?'

'Essential supplies.'

Clearly he wasn't going to tell her any more than that. She had no choice but to go with him as he shepherded her back to the office, waited for her to remove the wellies and boiler suit and change back into her usual clothes, then drove her to Cambridge and parked in the car park next to a shopping mall.

'Why are we here?' she asked.

'Because your clothes are completely unsuitable for the job. You can't garden in a business suit,' he said.

'But—'

'No arguments. What size are you?' When she didn't reply, he said with a casual wave of his hand, 'Fine, I'll guess.'

'No, wait.' His legs were so long that she was having difficulty keeping up with his strides.

As if he realised, he slowed his pace. 'Size?' he asked again as he shepherded her into a shop. She told him. And then he rapidly picked out three pairs of jeans, four T-shirts and the most revolting sunhat she'd ever seen.

'Why—?' she began.

He almost seemed to know what she was thinking, because he cut in, 'Because if it's sunny, you'll need protecting from the sun—you have fair skin and without a hat you'll burn. This isn't trendy or sexy, I know, but it'll be effective. That's more important.'

Before she realised his intention, he'd paid for the clothes.

'I'll reimburse you,' she said.

He shook his head. 'This isn't the sort of thing you'd normally buy, is it?'

Even so, nobody bought her clothes. Or chose them for her. Part of her was annoyed at the implied slur on her competence, but part of her was charmed. Will Daynes was looking after her. Cherishing her. Making her feel…special.

She couldn't remember anyone ever making her feel this way before.

'And if it makes you feel any better, I'll claim it as a business expense. You're shadowing me. This is equipment you need.'

'Clothes don't count as a bus—' she began, and then subsided when Will gently laid a forefinger over her lips.

'It doesn't matter. And I'm not exactly poor. I can afford this, Amanda. Go with me on this one.'

Her mouth actually tingled where he touched her. A tingle that spread over her skin until her whole body was very, very aware of his. It felt as if every nerve end was whispering his name, wanting him to stroke her and tease her and build up the desire until her climax burst through. For one mad moment she almost sucked the tip of his finger into her mouth.

Almost.

She managed to keep hold of her common sense. Just. But she couldn't speak. Dared not speak, in case she said something completely inappropriate. Something needy.

So there was only one thing she could do. Nod acceptance.

CHAPTER FOUR

IT FELT weird, wearing jeans. Amanda hadn't done that since her student days. And even then she'd been more likely to wear smart trousers than scruffy jeans. Although she owned a pair of trainers, she only used them in the gym. The ones Will had made her try on and then bought before she could argue were half-running shoe, half-casual shoe. Nothing like what she would have chosen for herself. But she supposed they were practical for walking around in a garden.

And they were marginally better than green wellies.

'Ready?' Will asked.

'Mmm.' She finished fiddling with the camera so it had a good shot of the kitchen table: they'd agreed that the seed-planting would be a good piece of film for Dee to edit. Then she eyed the kitchen table. 'I didn't think you were going to cover it with mud. Isn't it a bit—well—unhygienic?'

'Firstly, this isn't mud, it's compost. Secondly, there's plastic sheeting on the table. Thirdly, I'll scrub it before dinner. And, fourthly, if you really want to do it on the floor instead...'

What was it about Will that made all these pictures flash into her head? Of herself lying flat on the terracotta floor and Will leaning over her, his mouth dipping to tease hers?

'Do it' did *not* mean 'have sex'. They were *working*. It was time she got a grip. She really, really hoped she didn't look as hot and bothered on the camera as she felt.

'...then you'll end up with chronic backache and I'll have ab-solutely no sympathy for you,' he finished.

'You know best,' she said—a little more crisply than she'd intended, but that picture in her head had rattled her. Big time.

'Right. Firstly, we need to get the compost in the right state for planting.' He slanted her a mischievous look. 'I would say like making pastry, when you make the mixture into fine breadcrumbs, but I doubt you make pastry.'

'I don't eat it, either. Too much saturated fat,' she shot back.

He didn't look in the slightest bit abashed. 'Okay. What we're doing here is putting air into the compost and making it easy for a root system to start growing through it.' He demonstrated the action.

'Shouldn't we be wearing gloves?' she asked.

'No. They decrease sensitivity.'

Was he deliberately making *double entendres*?

She dragged her mind back to the task in hand. As if anticipating her next comment, he added, 'You wash your hands thoroughly afterwards and use a brush on your nails.'

'Oh.'

'No lumps. We want this to be fine and smooth, almost like dry sand…or didn't you ever play in a sandpit as a kid?'

Her teeth gritted; Will was way too close to the bone. Her mother had hated going to the park so Amanda had never gone to play on the swings and dig in the sand. They'd lived too far away from the beach to go for impromptu trips on the weekend. Playing in the sand had been… Well, what you've never had, you shouldn't miss, she reminded herself. She ignored the question and concentrated on working the lumps out of the compost.

Will sighed and came to stand behind her chair. He was so close that she could feel his body heat. 'You're leaning on the compost and squashing the air out. Try this.' To her shock, he took her hands, scooped up a mound of compost, then gently encouraged her to rub her palms lightly together.

'Remember, you're not trying to make it stick together. You're trying to get the lumps out,' he said, then returned to his own pile.

Amanda wished she wasn't wearing a T-shirt. Right now she could do with a really, really thick sweater. Or some armour-plating. Anything to hide the signs of her body's arousal before he noticed them.

This was crazy. She wasn't interested in Will Daynes. So why was her body reacting to him in this way? Why was her skin tingling where he'd touched her? Why could she still feel the warmth of his body against her back?

They worked in silence for a while, and then Will leaned over to inspect her compost. 'That's great. Well done. Next, we fill the pots.' He took two pots from the stack next to him. 'Don't squash the compost into it. Just let it fall in and end up in a mound. Then brush your hand lightly over the top.' He demonstrated with his pot. 'Your turn.'

Brush your hand lightly over the top...

Oh, lord. She really had to get her mind out of the gutter.

It bothered her, because she didn't usually fantasise about anyone. She never had time. There was always work, or something to focus on that would improve her mind.

And this was more like playing than work, which made her feel uncomfortable. A discomfort that grew when he demonstrated actually sowing the seed. She really *shouldn't* be having these kinds of thoughts. Watching his finger slide into the compost and wondering how it would feel sliding into her body instead...

It must be the country driving her crazy. She wasn't some sort of sex maniac. Never had been. She was sensible and grounded and...

Her mouth went dry as her eyes met his. He knew what she was thinking. She was sure of it. And, worse, she had a feeling that he was imagining the same scene. His palms flattening against her thighs, stroking them apart. His fingers playing along her sex, teasing and inciting until she was wet and almost crazy with the need to feel him inside her. His mouth...

Oh-h-h.

Somehow she managed to plant the seed and water it.

And then Will made it worse.

'Label it so you know what it is—the plant's name, the date sown, and your initials.' He handed her a pencil and a piece of plastic that reminded her of an ice-lolly stick with a pointed end. 'If you rub the top half between your finger and thumb, you'll feel that one side's rougher than the other. That's the side that's easier to write on.'

All she had to do was slide the plastic between her fingers. It was a perfectly innocent act. And yet it felt somehow...sexual. A come-hither kind of gesture. As if she were suggesting to Will that her fingers could stroke him in the same way.

She really, really, had to stop this. Focus. Get it back to business. 'What's the plant name?' she asked.

'*Helianthus*. Sunflower.'

Thank God for that. If it'd been the sort of plant Georgia O'Keeffe had painted, all sexy unfurling petals just waiting for a man's touch…

She quivered. No, no, no. She couldn't possibly desire Will Daynes. He was so laid back he'd drive her mad with frustration.

But, oh, the thought of how he'd soothe that frustration…

They finished planting the sunflowers; then, as he'd promised, Will took the plastic covering outside, shook the last bits of loose compost into the back garden, and scrubbed the table.

Odd about the back garden, she thought. It didn't look like a garden expert's garden—it didn't even have a greenhouse. And it was nothing like the designs he'd done for the garden centre. Maybe it was a case of not having time to look after his own backyard because he was too busy sorting out other people's.

'Can I help with dinner?' she asked.

'No, you're fine. Though you could pour us both a glass of wine, if you like. There's a bottle in the fridge.' He busied himself at the hob while she located the corkscrew and two wine glasses.

'Thanks,' he said when she handed him a glass.

'So, why did you become a gardener?' she asked.

'Why did you become an accountant?' he parried.

'I was good at maths and economics, so it made sense to go into a career in finance.' Plus it meant she'd never again have to live in a tiny village where everyone knew your business and you didn't fit in—where you were always found wanting because you weren't like everyone else. Never again would she feel a burden, knowing that she was the reason her mother hadn't been able to have the high-flying career of her dreams, because, after a career break, everyone would be too far ahead for her to catch up so there was no point in trying. The city was anonymous, nobody judged you, and Amanda liked it that way.

'So it was a decision you made with your head, not your heart?'

'Heart doesn't come into it,' she lied. Her heart had told her to run from the country as fast as she could, find somewhere that she'd fit in. And she'd been good at figures. She'd been so sure a career in finance would be right for her…

She suppressed the thought that maybe it wasn't. Of course it was. Figures meant common sense and no difficult emotions. You knew where you were with figures.

He raised an eyebrow. 'So if you had no restrictions on you, what would you do?'

'Be an accountant.' Stick with the safety of figures and calculations. 'What about you?'

'What I do now,' he admitted. 'I'd hate to be stuck in an office all day, having interminable meetings with self-important people who waffle on about nothing. Having to be at certain places at certain times and account for every second of my time.' He grimaced.

'Don't you have to do that at the garden centre? Have meetings and appointments, I mean?' she asked.

'It's not all day, every day. I don't know how you stand it, being stuck indoors all the time and never breathing in fresh air, hearing the birds sing or feeling the sunlight on your skin.'

'Let me see. The choice is working indoors in a nice, quiet environment where the temperature's just how I like it and coffee's nearby—or having to do heavy physical work when it's hot and sticky, not being able to feel my feet because it's so cold outside, and being soaked to the skin because it's bucketing down,' she countered. 'I know which I'd pick.'

'Hmm.' He sprinkled something into the pan, stirred it a bit, threw some scraps to Sunny, and then dished the contents of the pan on to two plates.

She took a mouthful. The peppery taste of rocket merged with the sweetness of the bacon, the nuttiness of the pearl barley and the saltiness of the parmesan. 'It's very good.'

'And it virtually cooks itself.'

Right. But if he thought she was going to cook this for him when he shadowed her... No way. They'd be eating out.

'So,' he said when they'd cleared their plates and he'd fed the dog, 'I suppose you'll go and find yourself a quiet corner and tell the camera all the things that are wrong with my lifestyle.'

'I'll tell you now, to your face.' She picked up the camera and switched it on. 'You want to know what's wrong with your lifestyle, Will? You have no sense of time. There's no order to your life—you value being spontaneous above everything else. You keep everything in your head.'

'And that's wrong *how*, precisely?' He folded his arms, looking at her with narrowed eyes. 'Flexibility's a business asset.'

That wretched word again. She shoved the thought aside. 'Yes, and if you can't be there for some reason, if you're called away urgently or you get the flu and you're in bed for a week—' bad choice of phrase; she had to swallow hard to suppress the thought of Will Daynes in bed for a week. In *her* bed for a week, all rumpled and sexy '—what does the rest of your team do?'

He shrugged. 'They're experienced enough to carry on. They know what they're doing.'

'But *how*, if you don't have anything planned? How do they know which client they need to be seeing, what stage the design is at, what materials you've already ordered, what still needs to be done?'

'They'll work it out.' He leaned back in his chair and spread his hands. 'It's a matter of trust.'

'Trust?'

'You have to trust people at some point, Amanda. Delegate. Let people use their initiative.'

Yeah, right. The last time she'd done that, there had been an unholy mess and she'd taken the flak for it. Nowadays, she checked everything herself.

'But you can't let yourself do that, can you? You need to be in control all the time. Look at your confidentiality agreement,' he said. 'Why did you feel you needed that?'

Wasn't it obvious? 'Because I deal with people's finances. Personal data. Most of what I do in my job is confidential.'

'I thought all company accounts had to be registered and visible for public inspection?'

'They are. But balance sheets and profit-and-loss accounts are only the end product.'

'I'm not with you.'

She sighed. 'Okay. Suppose you were going to bring in a new line of plants, and you were going to be the first people in the area to do it, maybe even the first in the country—that takes planning. And as your accountant I'd know about it.'

'How?'

'Because it'd be part of your budget and I'd have asked you what the money was earmarked for. If I gave those details to your competitor, so they could do exactly the same thing, but do it a month earlier, that would mean your advertising spend was wasted and your publicity would be out of date before you even started. It would have a knock-on effect on your business, too, because people who wanted those plants would visit your competitor instead of you, and maybe switch their entire business there.'

He was silent for a moment. 'I wouldn't divulge any details of your clients' business.'

She believed him. There was something solid and dependable and trustworthy about him. Will wasn't a man who'd lie or cheat. But… 'I can't take that risk,' she said softly. 'What about you? Why didn't you ask me to sign a confidentiality agreement?'

'I don't need one. As I said, you have to trust people at some point.'

She smiled wryly. 'You're so laid back, you're flatter than horizontal.'

He raised an eyebrow. 'So what's the alternative? Stress about things until I make myself ill?'

She made a noise of contempt. 'I don't stress about things.'

'No? You plan everything to the last detail.'

'There's nothing wrong with that.'

'And what if something changes? How do you cope with change?'

'I cope fine with change.'

His expression suggested that he thought otherwise. 'So what do you do to relax?' he asked.

'I go the gym on the way home.'

'And I bet you do a workout on your own.'

She stared at him. 'Meaning?'

'I can't see you working in a class. Letting someone else have control of what you do.'

'I'm not a control freak.'

'Aren't you? You gave me an itinerary about what we're going to do on your week. And I bet it's driven you crazy that I haven't done the same for you.'

'I think it's a little unprofessional, yes,' she said carefully.

He laughed. 'You need to learn to chill out, Amanda.'

'And you need to be more organised.'

'This,' he said softly, 'is going to be an interesting two weeks. And I'm going to teach you something you've maybe forgotten about.' He reached over and switched off the camera. 'Fun. And pleasure.'

She really wasn't sure whether that was a promise…or a threat.

CHAPTER FIVE

'SO WHAT do you normally do on a Saturday night?' Will asked when they'd finished washing up.

Amanda shrugged. 'Depends.'

'Would I be right in guessing "work"?' he asked.

She sighed. 'Don't give me a hard time about it. I get enough of that from Dee. Look, I know where I want my career to go, and I'm still at a level where that means putting in the hours to prove myself and get the experience I need. Is it so wrong to be committed to my job?'

'No. But there is such a thing as balance. And you're on my schedule, this week—so we're chilling out tonight.'

She looked slightly nervous. 'Please don't tell me that involves clubbing.'

He laughed and ruffled Sunny's fur. 'In the middle of the Fens? Hardly.'

'You're not that far from Cambridge.'

Fair point. Guilt twinged through him. She was closer than she thought, too—he often did go into the city. Because he lived there. Within a very short walking distance of the city centre, actually. Lying didn't come easily to him, but how could he tell her the truth without messing things up for Dee and Martin? 'I'm not a clubbing fan.' He much preferred the theatre and live music. 'We could watch a film, if you like.'

'At the cinema?'

'I was thinking more along the lines of watching a DVD here,' he said. 'We've already left Sunny on her own a fair bit today.' And if they went into the city, he'd probably leave the cinema on autopilot and end up outside his house with his front door key halfway towards the lock. Which would need a *lot* of explanations.

'Fair enough.' She coughed. 'Um, I meant to ask earlier. Is your girlfriend all right about this lifeswap thing and my staying here?'

He smiled. 'Are you asking me if I have a girlfriend, Amanda?'

'Only out of politeness.'

Politeness? Interesting that she was blushing, then. 'Since you're asking, I'm single.' He raised an eyebrow. 'And I'd guess you don't have time for a boyfriend.'

She lifted her chin. 'That's making assumptions.'

'But I'm right.' No question about it.

Her eyes narrowed. 'Don't be so smug.'

He pantomimed hurt. 'Smug? *Moi?*'

She didn't smile. 'Not that it's any of your business—I don't need a boyfriend.'

She'd already told him why, more or less. 'Because your career comes first.'

'Look, there's no law that says unless I'm going out with someone I'm an alien species.'

'You don't need to defend yourself to me,' he said softly. 'I understand.' Amanda was a lot like his mother—though he had a feeling she wouldn't make his mother's mistakes of settling down, having a family, then paying more attention to her career than her kids. Amanda would never have children in the first place.

'Is that why you're single?' she asked.

Because he was putting his career first, too? 'Sort of. I'm not ready to settle down yet.' He'd dated a fair bit—but he'd kept things light, and made sure his girlfriends knew that the relationship was for fun rather than for ever. Except his last girlfriend had been convinced she could change his mind, and had taken it badly when she'd realised she couldn't. The break-up had been messy enough to make him avoid dating for the last six months. Not that he intended to discuss that with Amanda. He changed the subject. 'So. Want to choose a film?'

She glanced at the single bookcase in the room. 'From where?'

He followed her gaze. There were a few battered paperbacks on the shelves, but that was all. Not even his taste; these were blockbusters, holiday reading for the cottage's usual holidaymakers. Another mistake. He should've thought to bring some films with him.

Served him right for lying to her.

He pushed the guilt away. 'The local video-rental shop's got a reasonable choice.' At least, it used to have, in the years when he lived around here. He really hoped there was a DVD player in the cottage or he was going to have to come up with a believable excuse. Maybe he could claim the player was broken and they'd have to play the film on his laptop. 'I've had only one glass of wine and a decent meal to soak it up, so I'm below the limit. I'll drive us into the village.'

While Amanda went to freshen up, he had a quick scout round. To his relief, there was indeed a DVD player, and a membership card for the local video shop. Well, it was what he'd expect from his uncle and aunt: making sure that their guests had everything they wanted. Like the massive folder full of local information and the visitors' book, both of which he'd temporarily moved to his room to avoid awkward questions from Amanda.

He slid the card into his wallet, and had Sunny sitting ready in the car by the time Amanda came downstairs again.

She was back in her business suit, he noticed. Was she just not comfortable with anything casual—or did she too feel that weird pull of attraction between them, and this was her way of reminding him that this lifeswap thing was strictly business? Not that he was going to ask. He simply drove them into the village.

'Choose whatever you like,' he said when they walked into the shop.

'I don't mind.'

He grinned. 'So I can pick a really gory slashfest movie, then?'

Just for a moment, her mask slipped and he glimpsed horror in her eyes. Then she was back to being polite ice-maiden. 'Of course. It's your house,' she said.

On loan for a week. Guilt flooded through him again. 'I was teasing. What sort of thing do you like?'

'Really soppy, girly films.'

Her delivery was so deadpan that he almost fell for it. Then he laughed, pleased that she'd relaxed enough to tease him back. Maybe these couple of weeks were going to work out okay after all. '*Touché*. I deserved that.' He slid his arm round her shoulders, squeezing gently before releasing her again—and was shocked to realise that, actually, he didn't want to let her go.

He knew he'd be mad to give in to the urge—they could both do without the complications. His head knew that Amanda was completely wrong for him. She hated the country as much as he loathed her world, she didn't share the same interests and she was a workaholic who'd always put him second to her career, the way his parents had. But his heart wasn't listening. Now he'd touched her, he wanted to hold her again. Closer, this time. Close enough to feel her heartbeat against his. Close enough to find out for himself if her hair felt as silky as it looked. Close enough to brush his mouth against hers and tease her until she opened her mouth and really let him kiss her, hot and wet and deep and—

Oh, he really had to get a grip. And a long, freezing cold shower might be a good idea, too. 'So what sort of thing do you really like watching?' he asked. 'Comedy? Serious drama? A weepie? An action movie?'

In the end, they settled on a critically acclaimed drama that had just been released, and Will bought a large bag of popcorn.

'I'm surprised you approve of popcorn, being such a foodie,' she said when they got back to the cottage and he tipped the popcorn into a large bowl.

'Of course I approve of popcorn. It goes with a film, doesn't it? Like ice cream. But I like my popcorn salted—better still if it's freshly cooked and still warm.' He slanted her a look. 'Though the ice cream has to be good-quality vanilla, not the cheap and nasty stuff that tastes of powder.'

She rolled her eyes. 'You're such a food snob.'

'No. Unlike you, I believe that food is more than just fuel. Which I guess is something else we can explore in this lifeswap thing,' he said. He settled in one corner of the sofa with the remote control, and patted the seat next to him. 'Come and sit down before I spill the popcorn everywhere.'

This was surreal. If someone had told Amanda she'd be watching a film and eating popcorn with a man she barely knew, on his sofa, with his dog stretched out on the floor at their feet, she'd have thought them crazy. She never just sat down and watched a film. There was always something to do, something new to learn that would give her that edge in business and make sure she never ended up in her mother's position, trapped in a world she hated. Why waste a couple of hours in front of the small screen?

And yet here she was, sitting on the sofa with Will, watching a film. Sunny was sprawled out on the floor, snoring happily. Amanda would normally have run a mile from this sort of situation, but somehow this felt…right.

'Help yourself,' he said, offering her the bowl. 'I'm perfectly capable of eating this all on my own—and you're too polite to stop me.'

Too polite? Hmm. He had a point. Maybe she was. She took a couple of pieces of popcorn, but she was aware of Will watching her. 'What?' she asked.

'I was just wondering…do you ever let go?'

'I don't need to,' she said quietly. 'And there's nothing wrong with being anchored. Stable.' She refused to let herself hear the word 'rigid'.

Will said nothing; it felt like a quiet criticism. She ignored it and settled down to watch the film. Every time she dipped her fingers into the bowl of popcorn, her fingers seemed to brush against his—the lightest, tiniest touch—and it felt as if every nerve in her body had been galvanised.

Weird.

This wasn't the sort of thing that happened to her. She was sensible, practical and efficient, not a dreamer. She was *not* going to start having fantasies about Will Daynes.

Yet she couldn't help giving him a sidelong glance—and blood scorched into her cheeks when she realised he was doing exactly the same. Glancing at her, those incredible eyes full of interest.

Was he wondering the same sort of thing that she was?

Just one tiny move. That'd be all it would take. All she had to do was let her lips part, tip her head back slightly in invitation, and he'd kiss her. She could see it in his eyes. And it would be one hell of a kiss. Enough to blow her mind and—

And she'd completely mess up this thing for Dee. She needed to remember why she was here. Not because Will had invited her here as his lover—because they were helping Dee with this project. This was business. She was going to count backwards from a hundred until her pulse slowed down again, and she'd keep some mental distance between them in the future.

When the film finished, even though she wasn't tired, Amanda yawned and placed her hand in front of her mouth. 'Sorry, Will. I'm shattered. Must be all the fresh air,' she fibbed.

'It usually makes people eat a lot and sleep a lot,' he said with a smile. 'See you in the morning. Sleep well.'

And what were his plans for tomorrow? She just about managed to stop herself asking. He clearly knew it, because there was the tiniest twinkle in his eyes. 'See you in the morning,' she echoed, and walked deliberately slowly. Just to prove she wasn't running scared of him.

In her room, she took up the camera and sat next to the window, where she could see the first few stars breaking through. Training the camera on her face, she began to speak, quietly yet precisely.

'I can't work him out. Will Daynes is passionate about what he does and he's a complete food snob—he's got high standards. And yet he drives around in a scruffy heap of a car and never seems to plan anything. I have no idea what such a strange mixture of a man could teach me, to make my work better. And I don't even know where to begin teaching him, because what he does is so far away from what I know, it's untrue. I know about planning and order. He does spontaneity and…well…untidiness. I think for a lifeswap thing to really work both people need to have more of a crossover in their lives. Will and I…we're just too opposite.'

She turned the machine off. What she didn't say out loud—and wasn't really happy about admitting to herself, even—was that Will Daynes was also the most intriguing, most attractive man she'd ever met. Worse, it wasn't just sex. There was something about him. And she was scared that if she got to know him better, she'd be halfway to falling in love with him. They were too different for it to end in anything but heartbreak. So it was better not to start anything.

She was going to be sensible about this. Absolutely sensible.

It took a long while for Amanda to fall asleep that night. Strange house, strange bed—and very, very strange sounds. There wasn't the quiet hum of traffic she was used to; here, the silence was broken every so often by a howl or a cry. Owls, foxes, bats... She shivered, despite the warmth of the night, and pulled the bed-clothes tighter.

She only realised she'd fallen asleep when she blinked and the room was full of sunlight through the thin cotton curtains. She glanced at her bedside clock and gasped in horror. It was almost ten o'clock. She never slept this late. Ever.

Will must already be awake; she could smell coffee.

Proper coffee.

Just what she needed to get herself functioning again, back to normal efficiency.

She showered, washed her hair, dressed and was downstairs in fifteen minutes flat. Will was sitting at the kitchen table, drinking coffee and reading the paper. Sunny was beside him, her head on his knee; Will was absently scratching the top of her head. Her tail thumped once when she saw Amanda; the noise made Will look up.

'Morning.'

Oh, lord. That smile was amazing. Imagine waking up to that every day... The idea sent a shiver through her. 'Morning,' she said, striving to sound cool and responsible and hoping she didn't sound as breathless as she felt.

The table was set for two, and it felt oddly domestic. As if she belonged. Which, of course, she didn't—she was a city girl through and through, and this was most definitely the middle of the country. A particularly *isolated* spot of the country. Worse even than the place where she'd grown up and been so miserable and lonely. You're just shadowing him for a week, she reminded herself. This isn't real.

He filled her mug from the cafétière and added a splash of milk—just how she liked it. Amanda was impressed that he'd remembered.

'Would you like a croissant? I picked some up from the baker's this morning.'

He'd left the house and she hadn't even heard his car? 'Thanks. I'm sorry for sleeping in so late.' She bit her lip. 'I must have for-gotten to set my alarm.'

'Listen to your body,' he advised sagely. 'It's telling you something.'

She groaned. 'You're not going all New Age on me, are you?'

He laughed. 'No, but I did warn you that the air around here makes people sleep longer than usual. Relax. It's Sunday morning and we don't have to rush about.'

'Sunday's usually your day off?'

'Yes and no.'

Infuriating man. Why couldn't he give her a proper answer? If she asked him for a straight answer, he'd probably say 'Roman road' or something equally facetious. If it wasn't for the look on his face when he talked about a garden or food, she'd say Will Daynes wasn't capable of being serious about anything.

While the croissants were heating in the oven, he raided the fridge for juice, and put butter and homemade jam on the table.

'Don't tell me—local farmers' market?' she asked.

'Don't get me started about food miles and carbon footprints and the importance of buying local produce in season. Fliss tells me I can be very, very boring.' He smiled at her. 'Let's just say this will be the best strawberry jam you'll ever taste.'

Three minutes later, she had to admit it. 'Gorgeous.'

When they'd demolished the plate of croissants, he said, 'Question for you. How many senses are there?'

She frowned. 'Five, obviously.'

'Which are?'

She wasn't quite sure where this was going, but she played along. 'Sight, hearing, touch, smell, taste.'

There was just the tiniest quirk of his lips. 'I'm surprised you didn't add "six, if you're gullible", with your views on New Age stuff.'

'Are you telling me now you're an old hippy?'

He laughed. 'No. The real question is, how many of your senses do you use in your job?'

She took a mouthful of coffee, hoping the caffeine would kick in soon because she really wasn't following this. 'I'm not with you.'

He picked up a camera very similar to the one Dee had lent her, and switched it on. 'How many of your senses do you use in your job?' he repeated patiently.

'Sight, obviously—I'm looking at figures. Hearing, if I'm listening to a client. Um…touch, as I'm touching the computer keyboard or turning pages in a file.'

He lifted his hand to stop her. 'Ah, no, there's a difference—you're pressing the keys, but you're not *touching* them.'

'That's illogical. Of course I'm touching them.'

'But you're doing it on autopilot. It's just a function. You're not registering the feel of the keyboard.'

She must have looked blank, because he asked, 'So are the keys on your computer smooth or slightly rough?'

She shook her head. 'No idea.'

'My point exactly.'

'That's trivial, Will. It's not *important* whether they're rough or smooth.'

'Yes, it is. The point I'm making is that you're not using all your senses. You don't notice texture.'

Lord, the way he said the word. It made her want to reach out and touch him. Explore the texture of his skin and find out if he felt as good as he looked.

'You also don't use smell or taste.'

Smell. He'd been close enough for her to smell his clean, personal scent earlier. And taste… Just how would Will Daynes taste? With difficulty, she dragged her eyes away from his mouth and her mind back to the point. *Business.* 'Not unless I'm doing an asset inspection or a stock-take and the stock happens to have some kind of scent. Tasting's not really on the agenda.'

'But your office has a scent. Whether it's dust—well, no, in your case no dust would dare to settle,' he corrected himself swiftly, 'or the scent of paper or ink or whatever plants grow in your office.'

She didn't think the plants in the office had a scent. There certainly weren't any on her desk. 'I don't *need* to smell or taste.'

'We'll prove that later,' he said, and switched off the camera again.

'I thought I was doing the filming, this week?' she asked.

'It's a two-way thing. Your impressions of my job—my impressions of how you'd cope with it.'

He'd already filmed his view of her—the way she had of him?

Part of her wanted to know what he'd said; and part of her thought it would be safer not to know.

'Next week, we swap over.' He topped up her coffee. 'Right, time for work.'

'We're going to the garden centre?' she guessed.

'No. I'm not there all the time. Today I'm working from home.' He walked over to one of the worktops, where she hadn't noticed a board leaning against the wall. He turned the board round to face her. 'What does this say to you?'

'It's a collection of pictures of gardens.' Completely haphazard. Some had ragged edges, as if they'd been ripped out of a magazine. Others looked like proper photographs.

'It's a mood board,' he explained. 'I ask my clients to look through magazines and newspapers and on the internet and collect pictures of gardens they like the look of.'

'So you make their gardens look like whatever they've seen in a magazine?'

He shook his head. 'I capture the mood—these are the sort of gardens that have the look and feel the client wants me to create for them.'

'What if the mood board is full of huge gardens, but they only have a tiny space?'

He smiled. 'Then we use clever planting to make a small space feel like a large one.' He rummaged in a cupboard and brought out a tray. 'Okay, imagine this is our small garden.' He grabbed items from the kitchen worktops and plonked them at random on the tray. 'How does it look?'

'An untidy mess,' she said without thinking.

'You are *such* a neat freak.' He laughed. 'Well, apart from untidy. What does the space look like?'

'Cluttered,' she said, 'and small.'

'Exactly.' He removed most of the items and arranged the others more carefully.

She couldn't help watching his hands, wondering how they'd feel on her skin. It drove her crazy.

'And now?'

He sounded completely businesslike—and she was grateful that these mad desires clearly didn't show on her face. She nodded. 'Less is more. I see.'

'And then there are gardens within gardens, for larger areas.'

'How does that work?'

'If they want the garden to do lots of different things, you can divide the space up. Have a place for the kids to play, an entertaining area, a formal garden and a place for just chilling out with a good book and a long, cold drink.' He smiled at her. 'Today, we're going to design a garden.'

'We?' But she knew nothing about gardening. Or design.

'You're shadowing me; the rules are, you're doing what I'm doing. Here's my report.' He handed her a plastic wallet filled with paper. 'If you can't read my handwriting, just yell and I'll translate.'

That wasn't a problem. His script was big and bold and spiky. An artist's handwriting, beautiful to look at and yet easy to read.

'And when you've read it, you can tell me what you think.'

'I don't know anything about gardens,' she reminded him.

'You know about analysing data, don't you? It's the same sort of skill—just different data, really.' He looked at her. 'Do you mind if I put some music on? I usually work to music.'

'Sure.' She preferred to work in silence, but she could tune it out. Unless he listened to really loud, intrusive stuff with a heavy bass.

'Thanks.' He took a laptop case out of a drawer in the kitchen, slid what looked like a very expensive piece of kit on to the kitchen table, and plugged an MP3 player into it. Soft piano music—something she didn't recognise, but actually rather liked—floated into the air.

'What's this?' she asked.

He gestured to the MP3 player. She glanced at the display, and was none the wiser. 'Fulham?'

'That's where the garden is.'

'Your playlist is called *Fulham*?' she asked in disbelief.

'My playlists are organised by gardens.' He fiddled with the player. 'Remember what I said about using all the senses? Sound helps to set the mood. Close your eyes and listen. What does this one make you think of?'

Classical guitar music, not quite flamenco, but getting that way. It made her think of hot afternoons under a Mediterranean sun. Lying in the grass in a field full of orange trees under a blue, blue sky. With Will propped on one elbow next to her, leaning over, his mouth about to—

Focus, she reminded herself. 'A Spanish garden?' she guessed.

'Near enough. A Mediterranean terrace,' he agreed. 'How about this? And keep your eyes closed, Amanda.'

Right now, she didn't dare open them. In case he was doing what she was just imagining, leaning over her with his mouth about to tease hers.

The sound of the Beach Boys floated into the air. She smiled. 'California. Palm trees and surf.'

'And what are they doing?'

'I don't know. Driving along the seafront? Finding waves or whatever it is surfers do?'

He laughed. 'Not in a garden.' He flicked to the next track in the playlist—an upbeat, summery, boppy track. 'This is for the same garden.'

'They're partying?' she guessed.

'More or less. This was a house with four kids aged nine to sixteen, and their friends came round a lot. So we're talking ball games, water fights, that sort of thing—we needed robust plants that could stand a ball being thrown into them, but which wouldn't end up with kids being covered in scratches or needing thorns taken out of their skin.'

In a weird way, this was starting to make sense.

'How about this one?'

Mellow, jazz-based music, a sultry-voiced female singer. Sunday-morning music. She suppressed the idea of waking up in Will's bed on a Sunday morning and making love to this record. 'A place to chill out,' she said. 'And nothing that needs a lot of looking after.'

He nodded. 'Well done. You're getting the hang of this. This was a rooftop garden in Docklands. A place to entertain on a Saturday night—and sleep off a hangover on Sunday morning.'

She wouldn't have a hangover, with Will. She wouldn't need to drink. His nearness was enough to make her dizzy.

'Go back to the first one,' she said. She listened for a while. 'It reminds me of raindrops.'

'It's Chopin's "Raindrop" prelude. Which means?'

'Water feature? Your client wants a fountain?' she guessed.

'Near enough. The garden backs on to the river.' He nodded to the file. 'Read, assimilate, and talk to me in twenty minutes.'

She felt the corner of her mouth quirk. '*You're* giving *me* a time limit?'

'Only because that's how you like working,' he shot back.

She read the file, glancing up at him every so often. He was clearly concentrating hard on whatever was on his laptop; his lips were very slightly parted and she could see the tip of his tongue caught between white, even teeth. In a faded black T-shirt and with that slightly too-long hair, plus the fact he clearly hadn't shaved that morning, he should've looked scruffy and a bit disreputable. Instead, he looked sexy as hell. Like a pirate. She could imagine him with a gold earring in one ear, and a red bandanna tied round his hair, and it made her knees weak. How easy it would be to reach across the small table and stroke his cheek, rub her thumb along his inviting lower lip, cup his chin and then touch her mouth to his...

Amanda was shocked to realise that she'd actually started to reach across towards him, and snatched her hand back. What on earth was wrong with her? She never got distracted like this at work. Several of her clients were good looking—probably more conventionally so than Will Daynes, because their hair was neater and they wore designer suits and shirts and ties—and she'd never once thought about kissing any of them.

It was just as well this lifeswap thing was only for two weeks. She could keep herself under control for two weeks, couldn't she?

Then she realised that Will was talking to her.

'Sorry. I missed what you said,' she admitted.

'Either that was the most boring file you've ever seen, or you're away with the fairies.' He laughed. 'And you don't have to be polite. Or answer that.'

'I was just surprised that your questions seemed to be—well—in a logical order.' Which was true. But it was also a million miles away from what she'd really been thinking about.

'If I don't ask, I don't find out what my clients need, and that means I can't give them what they want so I've failed in my job,' he said. 'Now, this is what we're working with.' He'd drawn a scale map, showing the aspect of the garden and its surroundings, and there were notes about the soil composition. The attention to detail surprised her—given Will's untidiness, she'd expected him to be a little more slapdash, taking the attitude that 'nearly there is good enough'. Instead, this was meticulous. Perfectionist. More the way she worked when she was detailing a client's systems.

Maybe they had more in common than she realised.

And clearly he knew his report by heart, because he talked her through building the garden, bouncing ideas off her and pointing out things on the mood board that he was going to adapt for the garden. He worked in pencil, she noticed, occasionally rubbing something out when a better idea occurred to him. And the end result was an incredibly detailed sketch.

'So there you have it. Your first garden,' he said with a smile.

It was hardly hers. 'You did most of it.'

'Teamwork, then.'

'I didn't exactly pull my weight,' she said.

'You did more than you think. You bounced some excellent ideas off me.' His smile broadened. 'But if you really want to do something for me...'

Down, girl, she warned her libido.

'...you can make us some lunch.'

CHAPTER SIX

'I DON'T cook,' Amanda warned Will.

'You don't have to cook salad. Well,' he corrected himself, 'not unless you're making a warm salad or you want to char the peppers first.'

'*Cold* salad I can do.'

'Okay.' His eyes were almost pure gold with mischief. 'The ingredients are in the fridge. I'll leave it up to you while I transfer some of these details to my computer.'

She opened Will's fridge and blinked. Nothing was in plastic boxes or bags, or shrink-wrapped: everything was in greaseproof paper or brown paper bags. A rummage in the salad drawer found her a lettuce with dirt still on it, wrapped in paper—a far cry from the bag of mixed leaves she was used to opening and tipping straight on to a plate. There was a red and an orange pepper, tomatoes in a brown paper bag, a cucumber that was clearly home-grown because it curved instead of being drainpipe-straight, and a brown paper bag of rocket.

Well, he'd set her a challenge—she had no intention of failing. Amanda didn't fail at anything, any more.

A bit of washing and chopping, and then she mixed the salad together in a large glass bowl. Will was a foodie, so she thought he'd expect something added on top.

Part of her wanted to give him the salad as it was—take it or leave it, because at the end of the day it was just fuel. But part of her wanted to please him. Wanted to make his eyes light up with pleasure. Wanted that sexy mouth to smile at her.

She poked about in the fridge and found a jar of olives and a hunk of parmesan. Although she spilled a bit of brine on the worktop, she managed to retrieve some of the olives from the jar and scattered them on top. The parmesan looked more like crumbled chunks than elegant thin slices, but it would do. There was a greaseproof packet filled with sliced ham, which she placed on a plate so they could help themselves.

'Lunch is ready when you are,' she said, looking over at Will.

And then she realised he'd been watching her. And he was smiling. Not quite the smile she'd had in mind. Was he laughing at her? She felt her eyes narrow.

His smile broadened. 'Don't scowl at me. It looks lovely. And I appreciate it even more because this isn't the sort of thing you normally do, is it?'

'No,' she admitted.

'Cooking's like gardening. You experiment. Try things out. If it doesn't work, it doesn't matter—you've learned something from it and know to try something different next time.'

She shook her head. 'It isn't like that in my job. You have to be accurate. There isn't any room for error—not unless you want to get a large fine for submitting false information.'

'That's a lot of pressure,' he observed.

She shrugged. 'I'm used to it.'

'Don't you ever think there might be something…more?' he asked softly.

'Like being stuck in a tiny village where everyone knows everyone else's business?' And where it was painfully obvious if you didn't fit in?

He didn't reply; he simply helped himself to the salad and started eating. 'Very nice,' he said. 'Thanks.'

She was fairly sure that he was feeding Sunny choice bits of ham under the table—but it was his house. It wasn't her place to tell him it wasn't hygienic.

'Did you sort your file?'

He nodded. 'We'll go and see the client tomorrow.'

'Don't you need to go to the garden centre?'

'I'm not there all the time,' he said, 'and the team's perfectly capable of getting on with what needs to be done.'

A level of trust she couldn't give her team. Not after the last time she'd trusted someone and then discovered, the day before the file was due in, that all the figures in a key section had been made up and she'd had to work through the night to fix it. She'd learned a lesson the hard way: as the senior on a job, she needed to spot-check her juniors' work.

'So, what's on the agenda for this afternoon?' she asked when they'd finished washing up.

Will glanced out of the window. 'Practical research, I think.'

She frowned. 'What's that?'

'Come and find out,' he invited. 'But you need to change first.'

Oh. So they were going to grub around in soil. She should've guessed that was what 'practical' meant.

'What you really need is a flowery dress and a straw hat,' he added, surprising her.

'Why?'

He shook his head. 'No matter. Jeans and a T-shirt will do fine. Remember the hat. And wear shoes you can walk in.'

Meaning the trainer-type things? Oh, wonderful.

By the time she'd changed, Sunny was settled in the back seat and Will had hooked up his MP3 player in the car. 'Today's a day for driving an open-topped car,' he said, sounding wistful.

'Your dream car?' she guessed.

He shook his head. 'I used to have one. It was way too small to fit much gardening equipment in the back. And, I...' He mumbled something into his hand.

'You what?'

'Got two speeding fines in the first week I had it,' he admitted, looking slightly rueful.

She could just imagine him in an open-topped sports car. Dark glasses, dressed completely in black, the wind ruffling his hair; just about any woman who saw him would melt into a puddle of hormones. And probably forget her fear about the fact he was driving way too fast. 'I see.'

'So I switched to a more, ahem, sedate model. One that suited a dog better, too.' He reached over to the back seat and ruffled Sunny's fur. 'Her mother, actually.'

'So you've had Sunny since she was born?'

He nodded. 'I still miss Sal—her mum—but Sunny's got the same sweet temperament. I can't work without a dog.'

Love me, love my dog. Yet another barrier between them. 'I suppose it goes with the territory. Being a countryman.'

'I suppose.' He shrugged. 'Want to choose some music?'

'Which garden do you suggest?'

He laughed. 'None. Try "Drive summer chill".'

It turned out to be slow, bluesy guitar music. Not the kind of stuff she was used to hearing on the radio on the rare occasions she switched it on.

As if guessing her thoughts, he said, 'I was brought up on Pink Floyd and Nick Drake by the original Sixties child.' His smile broadened. 'If you think I'm a hippy, you should meet him.'

'Your dad?'

For a moment, his face shuttered. Did that mean that his relationship with his parents was as strained as hers was with her own? 'Uncle,' he said.

His expression told her he didn't want to discuss it, so she let it be; she just listened to the music and watched their surroundings as he drove them into the city.

'Don't you need a permit to park here?' she asked, noticing a sign at the side of the road.

He stared at her in surprise for a moment, then seemed to shake himself. 'Good point. I always forget and I could do without a parking ticket.'

He parked in a nearby multi-storey car park, and sorted out Sunny's lead while Amanda got out of the car.

'So we're working in a garden in Cambridge?' she asked.

'No. Researching ideas,' he said.

Although she prided herself on her sense of direction, she would've been hopelessly lost in the maze of streets; Will seemed to know all the shortcuts and took her through narrow alleyways, past tiny cafés and second-hand bookshops, and finally through one of the colleges.

'This is the Backs,' he said. 'It's a bit touristy, but it's still beautiful. I thought we'd go on the river as it's the easiest way to see the gardens,' he said.

'Can't we walk?'

'Nope—the colleges own the river banks, so there's no public right of way.'

'What about Sunny? Will she be all right in a boat?'

The dog gave a soft woof, as if to reassure her.

'It's a punt, not a boat,' he said, and then his smile faded. 'Apart from the fact that she loves water, I'd never, *ever*, leave a dog locked in a parked car. People who do that should be locked up with the key thrown away for ever.'

There was a fierceness to his words that made her think this was personal. 'What happened?' she asked quietly.

'Let's just say that Sal's original owner was going to sue me for smashing his car window,' Will said, his voice soft and yet very, very dangerous at the same time.

So he'd rescued his first dog from an overheated car? Oh, lord. 'I…I don't know what to say. I'm a bit nervous around dogs, but I'd never hurt one.'

Will regarded her for a moment, then nodded. 'I know. And I'd rather not talk about it, if you don't mind. Let's just leave it that justice was done and he won't be owning another animal. Ever. Let's go hire a punt.'

'You know how to paddle?'

'Pole,' he corrected with a smile. 'I've done it a few times.'

A few minutes later, she was seated in the middle of the flat-bottomed boat, with Will standing on the flat platform at the end of the boat, wielding a long pole.

'Just lie back and relax,' he said. 'Or are you as nervous about boats as you are about dogs?'

'I'm not a coward,' she said, lifting her chin.

'I didn't say you were.' He eyed her curiously. 'So why are you scared of dogs?'

'This enormous Alsatian came up to me when I was three. Snapped at me.' She rubbed her arm without thinking. 'The owner stopped it before it could take a second bite, but I've still got the scar.'

'I'm not surprised you're scared. The dog probably would've been bigger than you, at that age,' he said thoughtfully. 'Didn't your parents try to get you to stroke a puppy or an old, quiet dog, to take away your fear?'

'My parents weren't into pets.' A neighbour had brought them a puppy, but her mother had refused to keep it, citing Amanda's fear of dogs, but Amanda had overheard her mother complaining to her father that night about 'yet another tie'.

'Shame. I was lucky—Martin and Helen have always had at least two dogs and three cats.'

Again, no mention of his parents, she noticed. He sounded closer to his uncle and aunt.

He nodded at Sunny. 'She's great with kids. Though she does have a bad habit of stealing shoes.'

'I'll remember to keep mine out of the way.' Though, looking at the spaniel's huge brown eyes and soft mouth, she couldn't imagine Sunny actually chewing anything.

She glanced up at Will again. He'd taken off his shoes, she noticed, and was actually punting in bare feet. He reminded her more and more of a pirate.

And he had the sexiest feet she'd ever seen. Well shaped and clean and... 'Um—is that safe?' she asked, to cover her confusion.

He smiled. 'It's how I've done it since I was a student.'

'You were a student here?'

'No. I spent a lot of time around here in the holidays. Now, we're going from Silver Street Bridge down to the quayside at Magdalene and back again,' Will said. 'This first bridge is the Mathematical Bridge at Queens' College.' He laughed. 'Some of the tour guides will tell you that Isaac Newton built it—then the story goes that the Fellows and students took the bridge apart and couldn't put it back together, and that's why it looks so rickety and twisty.'

She turned round to glance at the bridge. 'So what's the truth?'

'Newton died over twenty years before it was built and he went to Trinity, not Clare. And think how big and heavy the pieces are.'

She studied it. 'Not easy to take apart.'

'It's built according to a mathematical analysis of the forces in it. Clever stuff.' His smile broadened as she turned to face him. 'I just think it looks pretty, especially in spring when all the crocuses are out. It's like a sheet of deepest purple covering the bank. It's lovely in winter, too, when the trees are draped in frost.'

He really adored this place: it was obvious in the way he talked about it and the look on his face. 'This is Clare. The Fellows' garden there is fantastic. Mind you, so is the one at Christ—that was Milton's favourite garden.'

Such a casual namedrop. She knew who Milton was, of course—she just hadn't studied him. She had a feeling that Will knew just about any fictional or poetical garden, and could quote accordingly. His deep, slightly posh voice would sound amazing, quoting poetry.

There was something decadent about leaning back against the cushions, watching Will propel the punt along—and she had to admit, he was good at it. Really good. She felt perfectly safe here.

Then she remembered her earlier vision of him as a pirate. He could be a pirate right now, taking her back to his ship…

No. To lighten the mood—and to stop her thinking about how even looking at Will made a little knot of lust tighten in her stomach—she asked, 'Ever thought about being a gondolier?'

He laughed. 'If you really want me to sing "*O Sole Mio*…"' Actually, that's timely, because this is the Bridge of Sighs.'

'I thought the Bridge of Sighs was in Venice?'

'This one's built in the same style. That's how it got its name.'

'And you prefer the Cambridge one.'

He smiled. 'Yes. I love this city. Even though it's impossible to park and it's always full of students on bicycles. I love the fact the city's full of green spaces—and they don't let you walk on the grass in the colleges, so it *stays* green. I love the Botanical Garden, too. I might take you there later in the week.'

'Won't we be too busy working?'

'It counts as work. Background research,' he said. 'As does this.'

She scoffed. 'We're messing about on the river.'

'We're multi-tasking,' he corrected.

'Like how?'

'As you said, we're messing about on the river. Relaxing on a Sunday afternoon. But it's also educational,' he said. 'I brought you here to see the gardens, to look at how they work against the backdrop of the river. Which means that while you're lying there like a princess…'

He thought she was a spoiled brat? She glanced quickly at him. No, there was no censure in his expression. And this had been his

idea, anyway. He was just teasing. That hot look in his eyes was
her imagination, it was more of that stupid daydream about him
being a sexy pirate about to take her off to his lair and have his
wicked way with her.

'What do you mean, princess?'

'Queen, even. "The barge she sat in, like a burnish'd throne…"'
He gave her another of those hot looks, and her temperature went
up a couple of degrees. What would it be like to lie back against
the cushions with him leaning over her, that sensual mouth tracing
over her skin until she forgot where and even who she was?

'You said this was a punt, not a barge.'

'Nicely corrected.'

There was a teasing glitter in his eyes; she just hoped he
hadn't guessed why she'd said it—to stop herself leaping on
him.

'Back to business. I brought you here so you can have a think
about the garden we designed this morning,' he continued. 'Would
you change any of it, now that you've seen what they can do here?'

She listened, fascinated, as he pointed out buildings of interest
and features of the gardens he particularly liked, then told her about
the narrow little streets in the town and the markets and the anti-
quarian bookshops and the offbeat museums.

'If you ever get fed up with gardening, you could be a tour
guide,' she said, when they returned to the quay at Magdalene.

He laughed. 'I'll never get fed up with gardening. And I'd get
bored, having to repeat myself over and over again. I like the
challenge of the new.'

Was he warning her that he saw her as a challenge? Or was
he warning her that she wouldn't be able to keep his attention
for long enough?

He helped her out of the boat, and her arm tingled where he
touched it. If he had this effect on her with such an impersonal
touch, what on earth would it be like if he touched her more inti-
mately? If he undid her shirt and stroked every inch of skin as he
uncovered it. If he unclipped her bra and let her breasts spill into
his hands. If he slid his hands under the hem of her skirt and
smoothed her skin all the way up to the top of her thighs, and—

Oh, Lord. Slow, heavy desire throbbed through her at the thought.

And she really, really hoped he couldn't read her mind.

'Come on. I think Sunny could do with a walk—let's go out to Grantchester for afternoon tea,' he suggested.

'Where's Grantchester?' she asked.

'It's a village on the upper reaches of the river. Do you know the Rupert Brooke poem about lilacs being in bloom, the church clock standing at ten to three, and having honey for tea?'

She shook her head.

Softly, he quoted a few lines from the poem. And she was very glad they were leaning against the bridge, because her knees went decidedly weak. She'd been right in her earlier guess: Will could quote poetry about gardens from memory. And, with a gorgeous voice like his, Lord help her if he ever started quoting love poetry. She'd be a puddle of hormones within seconds.

'It sounds lovely,' she said, hoping the shivery feeling didn't show in her voice. 'Is it far?'

'No. A couple of miles, that's all.'

What she'd forgotten was that Will was used to walking a lot. She wasn't. Even though she worked out at the gym, she wasn't used to tramping down a country path. Forty minutes later, she felt hot and out of sorts—how was it possible to feel so sticky and fed up, when the cool clear water was running alongside them? Every so often she saw a punt glide past, and she wished she'd asked him to punt them up the river rather than walk all this way.

'Let's sit down a minute,' he said.

He'd noticed that she was struggling? Pride kicked in and she straightened her back. 'I'm all right.'

'Course you are. But I want to show you something. Well, not *show* exactly…but we need to sit still for this.' He sat on the bank, then lay back with his arms cushioning his head. Sunny nestled close to him.

For a second, Amanda actually thought about doing the same on his other side, resting her head against his shoulder and curving her arm round his waist and cuddling into him. And one of his arms would slide down to cradle her closer…

Then she pulled herself together and just sat on the bank next to him.

'Lie back,' he instructed, 'so you can see the sky. Look up through the trees.'

Sunlight slanted through the leaves and dappled the ground around them. It was a tiny piece of paradise, the air full of birdsong and the river running gently by them and the fields stretching out flatly to reveal a huge expanse of sky. A place where lovers had no doubt stopped to kiss, she thought. And when Will raised himself up on to one elbow, for a crazy moment she thought he was going to lean over, dip his head and brush his mouth against hers. Just as she'd imagined him doing under the Spanish orange trees he'd conjured into her mind.

Worse—she wanted him to. She really, really wanted him to kiss her. Here, in this perfect space. She could feel her lips parting and her eyes closing and...

'What can you hear?' he asked softly.

He wasn't going to kiss her. This was about the senses, not about sensual. A tiny shift in semantics, but one that made a huge difference.

And she was shocked to realise how disappointed she felt.

'Amanda?'

She swallowed hard. 'Birds singing.'

'Can you hear anything specific?'

She had no idea what she was supposed to be listening for. And she really didn't want him to guess what she'd just been thinking, so she grabbed the camera to put a barrier between them and started filming him. 'What should I be listening for?'

'Can you hear a bird singing something that sounds like "Did he do it? He-did-he-did-he-did?"' Will asked.

She paused, hoping that the camera was picking all this up. 'I think so.'

'That's a songthrush,' he said. 'And then there's the great tit— it sounds like a squeaky wheelbarrow.'

She listened, and heard the pause-and-squeak he'd told her about. 'Oh—yes!'

'Listen harder,' he said softly. 'Can you hear that little frrrrr sound, almost like a firework fizzing?'

She paused. 'Yes—just there.'

'That's a greenfinch,' he said.

'How do you know all this?' she asked.

'You listen for the sound and then you look around to see which bird made it.'

'I wouldn't even know where to start.'

'Just listen,' he said softly.

And amazingly, what she'd thought of as just background noise seemed to separate out—she could hear different songs. 'What's that one that sounds a bit like a bored lift attendant saying, "Going uuup, going uuup, going up now"?' she asked.

'Another blackbird.'

She stopped filming him. 'You know, you'd be a natural on TV.'

He shook his head. 'Not my thing. I like my life as it is.'

'You could teach people a lot.'

'I sometimes go into Fliss's school and do a workshop with the kids,' he said. 'It makes them think a bit about their environment. We plant sunflowers in the summer term, then harvest the seeds in the autumn term and make birdfeeders.'

She could see him doing that. Will Daynes would be brilliant with children; she could imagine him teaching children about plants and minibeasts and birds.

Shockingly, she could actually imagine him with children of his own. With a dark-haired girl and a little boy with her own colouring… The vision took her breath away. What on earth was wrong with her, imagining him with *her* children? For goodness' sake. Nothing was going on between them. And she most definitely wasn't planning to settle down and have children. That wasn't what she wanted. At all. She wasn't going to make the same mistake her mother had, ending up trapped in a cottage in the country with a child she didn't want.

'Ever thought about lecturing?' she asked.

'I'd be stuck indoors most of the time and I'd *loathe* it. I need to be outside,' he said simply. 'Though I do have links with one of the local colleges—some of their students do their work experience with me. They do a bit of casual work for me in the holidays or at weekends, too.'

No wonder he'd found it so easy to teach her about gardening. He'd done this countless times before.

And she was beginning to think that there was nothing at all she could teach him.

'Come on. I want a cup of tea. And some cake,' he said, getting to his feet in one lithe movement. He held out a hand to pull her up. Again, her skin tingled where he touched her. But he didn't seem in the slightest bit affected by the skin-to-skin contact, and no way was she going to let him know what it did to her. She didn't want him to think she was needy.

When they reached the village, he ordered them afternoon tea in a little café, and found them a chair underneath apple trees.

Tiny sandwiches were served along with gorgeous cake; Sunny, once she'd had her fill from a water bowl, lay between them, looking hopeful. On impulse, Amanda took the ham out of her sandwich. Will had said that Sunny was gentle, that she wouldn't snap or hurt her…and Amanda was charmed at how gentle the dog was when she took the ham from Amanda's fingers. And at how the dog licked her fingers, as if to say thank you.

'She's suckered you, then,' Will commented with a smile.

Amanda felt her eyes widen. 'Sorry. I should've asked you first.'

'No worries. Like all spaniels, she's incredibly greedy. A bit of ham won't do her any harm.' He ruffled his dog's fur. 'I'm glad she's helping you with your fear of dogs,' he added softly.

Yeah. That was one thing she'd be able to take back from this week—she wasn't scared any more.

Of dogs, that was. Because when they returned to the car she realised she hadn't looked at her watch once all day. Will had made her forget the importance of time. And that was a very, very dangerous thing.

CHAPTER SEVEN

WILL LAY back against the pillows, staring out of the window. The cottage wasn't overlooked, so he hadn't bothered closing the curtains at the window with a view on to the garden; he enjoyed watching the sky darken and the stars slowly wheeling round.

But tonight he wasn't seeing the constellations. The picture in his head was of Amanda, lying back against the grass in Grantchester Meadows earlier that afternoon, her eyes closed and her mouth very slightly parted. He'd been propped up on one elbow. How easy it would've been to lean over, dip his head and steal a kiss.

She had a beautiful mouth. A perfect rosebud. And he'd just bet she had no idea how tempting it was. Or how the soft cotton of her T-shirt had settled against her body, revealing curves he wanted to smooth with his palms and tease with his fingertips. He'd wanted to see her hair mussed by the grass, her mouth reddened with passion, her head tipped back in abandonment as he touched her, stroked her, teased her, and brought her nearer and nearer to the edge.

Or maybe she *had* guessed. Maybe that had been why she'd suddenly grabbed the camera and filmed him talking about birdsong.

He'd talked about one of the senses. Sound. But that hadn't been the uppermost one in his mind. His fingertips had been tingling, yearning to touch her skin and find out just how soft it was. And his mouth had wanted to know exactly how she tasted. He'd wanted to breathe in her scent, hear the change in her voice and her breathing as her arousal grew. See her pupils dilate and the ice-blue of her eyes sharpen with desire.

He knew she didn't do relationships. Neither did he, right now. And a relationship with her was out of the question, anyway—he loathed her world, the people and the attitudes and the brittleness. But he was beginning to think that a short, mad affair might be the best way forward; if they could get the physical attraction out of the way, they'd be able to concentrate on business.

Tomorrow, he'd find the right moment—and suggest it.

The next morning, Will woke to the smell of coffee. He glanced at the clock. It wasn't even seven yet. He had a nasty feeling that Amanda was one of these women who was at her desk before eight in the morning and didn't leave until almost eight at night. He showered swiftly, dragged a comb through his hair, dressed at the speed of sound and came downstairs to find her sitting at the kitchen table, working on a laptop computer.

But just as he was about to make a rude comment about workaholics, he noticed that Sunny was sitting with her head on Amanda's knee, and Amanda was fondling the dog's ears with her left hand. And Amanda was actually dressed for his kind of work—in jeans and a T-shirt.

Was he in some kind of parallel universe? Amanda was a buttoned-up businesswoman who was afraid of dogs. But the woman sitting at the kitchen table was someone else. Someone warmer. Softer.

Someone he could lose his heart to, if he wasn't careful.

His head knew that she was absolutely Miss Wrong. So why was he getting that warm feeling in the pit of his stomach every time he looked at her? Why did the ends of his fingers tingle with the need to touch her?

He became aware of a humming noise. 'What's that?' he asked.

'The washing machine. The weather forecast says it's going to be good today. Might as well put the washing out to dry before we go out—it'll save messing about with the dryer, later.'

His eyes narrowed. 'You've done the washing.'

She shrugged. 'There was enough to make a load.'

'My washing as well as yours?' The idea of her clothes tangling with his made him think about her limbs tangling with his. Very pleasurably. It was exactly what he'd dreamt about for what seemed like the whole of the previous night.

'And the towels. More efficient that way.'

The word broke the spell. No, he wasn't in a parallel universe. *Efficient*. That was Amanda all over. Efficient, organised—an ice maiden who was so far removed from her senses, it was untrue. He sat down and poured himself a mug of coffee from the cafétière; Sunny padded over to him and rubbed her nose against his knee.

'So what are you working on?' he asked.

'The client questionnaire. You know, you could save a lot of time by emailing your client a list of the questions you need to ask and getting them to start filling them out in advance.'

She was organising him. Putting a structure in place. He'd bet she'd even tried grouping the questions together in what she saw as a logical order—gleaned from the file on the design they'd worked on together the previous day, and the file he'd given her as bedtime reading. 'I hate to burst your bubble,' he said softly, 'but I've tried that already. And I've found that what they write on a questionnaire often isn't the same thing at all as what they really want. It's head stuff rather than heart stuff.'

'How do you mean?'

'They write down what they think they should have, not what they really want. It's only when they're chatting to me and say that they'd really love such-and-such a feature but they know their garden's too small that I can show them how to scale things down or create the same kind of effect with different plants.'

'I see.'

He noticed the glimmer of disappointment the second before she masked it. And he couldn't help reaching out to squeeze her hand. Just briefly. Comforting her. Even though the touch of her skin made his whole hand tingle with awareness. 'Hey. It was a good thought. Though I thought accountants were all about—well—figures?'

'Business systems, too. Making things work efficiently so the client can concentrate on the important bits of their job instead of getting bogged down in paperwork.' She smiled wryly. 'I've worked with personal tax clients who just bring me a shoebox full of receipts to sort out at the end of the tax year. And they're panicking they might've lost something important.'

'Uh-huh.' He knew that feeling. It had happened to him, a couple of times. Filing had never been at the top of his agenda.

'So I've set up an easy system for them—a concertina file, where one pocket's for stationery and another's for travel, and so on. At the end of the month they just drop the contents of each pocket into an envelope, seal it and write the name of the month and the title of the pocket on the front, and that saves a lot of time sorting through. It means their accountancy bill's lower because we don't have to spend so much time sorting out the files, and they don't have to worry about whether they've lost anything. Just a tiny, tiny bit of organisation and it's so much less stressful for them.'

'It means your company loses out on billing hours,' he pointed out.

'But if I left things as they were, we wouldn't be giving the client the best-value service. And that's dishonest. Wrong.'

She might be bossy and a control freak, but she meant well. The last remnants of his irritation vanished, replaced by a twinge of guilt. Honesty was important to her. And he'd been lying to her. It was for the best of reasons, but it was still lying.

Maybe today he'd find a way of telling her the truth, without making a complete hash of it.

'So is there a schedule today?' she asked.

'We're seeing my client at ten to discuss the plan, then going out to see another client to start the groundwork for a design that's already been agreed.'

'Is Sunny coming with us?'

'Not today. If it's going to be hot, she'll find travelling miserable.' He fondled the dog's ears. 'But I promise I'll take you on a long walk in the Fens as soon as we get home,' he said softly to the dog.

When they'd sorted out the washing and he'd loaded his car with the tools he needed, they set off.

And although Will knew that Amanda didn't watch much television, he was quite prepared for the shock of recognition in her face when his first client opened the door to them—a high-profile actress in a long-running television series.

Will had said he was a garden designer. He hadn't told her the half of it! Landscaping consultant to the rich and famous, more like.

'Why didn't you warn me?' she asked when they were back in the car.

'What?'

'Your client. She's *famous*. I mean, even *I* know who she is, and I don't watch the show! I can't believe you didn't make me sign a confidentiality agreement.'

'No need. I trust you.'

'And if you wake up on Friday and see it splashed all over the gossip mags?'

He shrugged. 'I'll deal with it if it happens. Though I don't think it will.'

He trusted her that much?

Clearly he did, because after a quick sandwich in a nearby pub he drove them to St John's Wood and introduced her to the client whose garden they'd be working on that week. The woman's surname meant absolutely nothing to Amanda—but the framed photographs of her husband were definitely familiar. It was a face she'd seen on the news. A lot.

'This place belongs to a famous footballer!' she hissed when they were in the garden.

'And?'

Will seemed completely unperturbed. Not in the least bit starstruck.

'Are you *sure* you don't want me to sign a confidentiality thing?'

'Yup.' He smiled at her. 'Though you might want to stick this fork in me by the end of the day,' he added, handing it to her. 'This is London clay.'

'What's wrong with clay?'

He bent down and scooped up a handful. 'See how it rolls into a ball and keeps its shape? That means there aren't many air spaces and it doesn't drain well.'

'So it gets waterlogged?' she guessed.

'In winter, yes; and in summer it's rock hard. So what we have to do is dig in some good organic matter to improve the soil crumb and drainage. The good news is, it holds nutrients better than other types of soil. It's brilliant for roses—which is just as well, as they want a rose arbour here.' He gave her a sidelong look. 'We have one other teensy problem.'

The way he said it made her realise it was a big problem. 'What's that?'

He pulled a leaf from a plant and showed it to her. 'Ground elder. It spreads like crazy, it doesn't die off in the winter and the only way to get rid of it is to dig up every single tiny piece of root.' He handed her a pair of padded gloves. 'You'll need these. You're not used to digging, so if your hands start to feel at all sore I want you to stop. Don't be stubborn about it,' he warned, 'because blisters aren't pleasant. And you need to stop every fifteen minutes to have a drink of water.'

Will—the most laid-back, spontaneous man she'd ever met—was working to a schedule? She couldn't help asking in disbelief, 'You're actually planning in breaks?'

'Just making sure you don't dehydrate, as it's such a warm day. I don't want you overdoing things and getting ill.'

He was looking after her. As any boss would look after a team, she reminded herself. As she looked after her own team, by making sure they had a proper lunch break—even if she didn't—and were clear about their tasks and knew to come to her if they were stuck.

But with Will, things seemed *personal*. As if he really cared.

When he made Amanda stop for a drink, he also made her take off the gloves and show him her hands. 'Hmm,' he said. He ran his fingers very lightly over her palm at the base of her fingers—weirdly, it felt as if he was stroking her spine and it made her want to purr with pleasure.

'Does that hurt at all?' he asked.

'No.' Her voice sounded croaky, even to her own ears, and she really hoped he'd put it down to a dry throat—one caused by thirst, not desire.

'Good. The second you feel even the slightest twinge, I want you to stop.' His mouth compressed. 'This is hard work, especially in this sort of soil. It's too much to expect you to do. I'll find you something easier.'

He was offering her a cop-out? No way. She didn't want him thinking she couldn't cope with any challenge he threw her way. And this whole week was about flexibility, wasn't it? She lifted her chin. 'I'm shadowing you. So I'm doing what you're doing.'

'Remember, I'm used to this and I'm bigger than you are. This isn't a competition, Amanda,' he said softly. 'It's all about teamwork.'

Teamwork. Funny how that word made her insides glow.

'You're doing well—especially for a gardening rookie,' he said, and drained his glass of water.

She followed suit. 'Let's blitz the ground elder.'

She watched him surreptitiously as he dug. The way he moved was almost like a ballet dancer—graceful, sure and strong. It was just as well he hadn't taken his T-shirt off because, half-naked, he would be more than tempting.

No doubt their client thought so, too, because she kept popping down to see them. She hardly bothered speaking to Amanda, but Will got the full-wattage smile and the breathy little voice and the batted eyelashes—false ones, too, Amanda noted.

Surely he could see the woman was flirting with him? After all, who on earth wore designer high heels and floaty cocktail dresses and full make-up when they were just pottering about in the garden?

'What?' he asked when the client had sashayed back to the house.

'I didn't say a word.'

'You didn't have to. You look immensely disapproving.'

Amanda stared at him. 'Well, she's married.'

'Uh-huh.'

'She's *flirting* with you, Will.'

'And that's a problem?'

He didn't sound in the slightest bit bothered. Well, he was probably used to women falling at his feet. He probably flirted all the time—though he hadn't really flirted with Amanda.

Not that she was jealous.

At all.

She resolved to say nothing, and kept digging.

Then she became aware that Will's hand was resting on the shaft of her spade; she stopped and looked up at him.

'Just for the record, Amanda, I believe in fidelity. I'm single, but she's not. Flirting's harmless. I don't mind having a laugh with my clients. But if she actually propositioned me, it would be a dif-

ferent matter and I'd make sure I was never here on my own with
her again,' he said softly. 'I'm here to do a job, and that's all: to
make this a dream garden. If she's having Lady Chatterley fantasies to go with it, they'll just have to stay in her head, because I
have absolutely no intention of acting them out for her.'

Amanda felt the colour flood into her cheeks. 'Oh.'

'And just to make sure we're clear on that…' He stripped off
his gloves, cupped her face in both hands, and brushed his lips
lightly against hers. Once, twice…

His mouth teased hers, nibbling gently at her lower lip until,
with a sigh, she opened her mouth. And then the kiss deepened
and her senses went into overload. She knew her eyes were closed,
but she could see coloured lights and hear the birds singing. She
could smell the sweet, loamy scent of freshly dug earth and feel
the sun warming her skin. And Will's mouth tasted tangy, of cool
lemon and warm man.

Just as unexpectedly as it had started, the kiss stopped.

'Why did you do that?' she asked, her voice a husky whisper.

'Because our client is standing at her French windows, watching us. Now she'll think you're not just shadowing me, you're
involved with me as well, and that will put me off limits as far as
she's concerned. She's not going to give me a blatant come-on in
front of my girlfriend. My lover,' he added in a voice so husky it
made her knees weak.

His eyes were the most peculiar colour. Almost like molten
silver. Sexy as hell. And she was shocked to realise she wanted him
to kiss her again. For one crazy moment she nearly reached up to
pull his head back down to hers and demand a replay.

'Expect huffs from her for the rest of the day—but there won't
be any more flirting. Okay?'

No. She didn't feel okay at all. Her head was spinning. *Will
Daynes had just kissed her*. It had been the most spectacular
kiss of her life—but from the coolness of his tone and the way
he'd replaced his gloves and gone back to digging out the
ground elder, it had meant nothing to him. Nothing at all. It had
all been for show. To make the client think that Amanda was
his lover.

His lover.

Of course she wasn't. But now the idea was in her head, it wouldn't go away. What would it be like to be Will's lover? To find out where he liked being touched, where he liked being kissed? To have him explore her with the same intensity and passion he gave to his other love, gardening?

Oh-h-h.

'Okay,' she lied, and resumed her battle with the weeds.

That kiss had definitely been a mistake, Will thought. He really shouldn't have done it. He'd annoyed his client—she'd been very terse with them both when she'd brought out a jug of cold drink—and he'd made Amanda wary of him. She'd avoided all eye contact ever since; she hadn't even looked at him when they'd stopped for a drink. So much for his earlier idea of suggesting a mad, short-lived affair. It was completely out of the question. There was no way she would consider it.

The kiss hadn't sated his desire for her either. It had made it a hundred times worse. Now he knew what it was like to kiss her, he wanted to do it again. And again, until neither of them could speak coherently.

Well, he'd just have to exercise a bit of self-control.

The journey from London to Cambridgeshire took a long, long time, Amanda thought. Will didn't bother making conversation; he just put some music on. Music that maybe relaxed him, but made her feel taut as a wire. It was music with a sensual beat—the sort of songs she could imagine in the background as they made love.

Not that she was going to make love with him.

She didn't do casual relationships, and she most definitely wasn't in the market for marriage and babies and having to put her career second. She'd seen what that had done to her mother. It wasn't going to be the same for her.

At last they were back at the cottage. Sunny bounced around the kitchen, clearly delighted to see him again, and Will made a huge fuss of her. Then, without actually making eye contact, he said to Amanda, 'The bathroom's all yours.'

Good. Maybe she could scrub this ridiculous desire away.

'What about you?'

'I'm used to digging. A shower'll do me fine. Don't rush—let the water soak the ache out of your muscles.'

And if it didn't, would he offer to knead the soreness out himself?

Uh. Bad thought. It was only one step from kneading her muscles to stroking her skin, and one step from stroking to caressing, and one step from caressing to—

She realised that he was talking again, and hoped he wasn't waiting for a response. She didn't have a clue what he'd just said.

'Take as long as you like,' he said. 'I'll cook dinner when you're ready—and in the meantime I'll take Sunny for a walk.'

A bath full of bubbles. She never lounged around like this; a shower was more efficient after a long day at work or a session at the gym. But it felt good to have the hot water melting away the strains of an afternoon's digging.

It would be even better if she could stop reliving the moment he'd kissed her. The feel of his mouth against hers. The way he'd coaxed her into kissing him back.

Maybe she should break her personal rule and suggest it. A mad, crazy, one-night stand to get this thing between them out of their systems, and then they could concentrate on Dee's project.

But if he turned her down…she'd never be able to face him again.

Annoyed with herself, she climbed out of the bath, dried herself, and dressed in clothes more within her comfort zone—a business suit. Just to remind herself that things between her and Will were strictly business.

She walked into the kitchen at the same time as he did.

'You look hot,' she said—then realised her words could be taken to mean something she hadn't intended. Not consciously, anyway.

'It's boiling outside. I could do with a long, cold drink,' he admitted. 'Join me?'

'I'll make it,' she said.

Funny how they'd slipped into a routine—she sorted the drinks while he cooked.

'Let's eat outside tonight,' he suggested.

Weird how it felt so intimate, she thought as she carried the cutlery and drinks through to the patio. The garden had only low fencing around it, and she could see the land stretching for miles around. Yet it felt as if they were in a tiny, tiny space.

It was probably her imagination. He'd kissed her, yes—but it had been for show, to get a message across to his client. It was not because he, Will Daynes, wanted to kiss her, Amanda Neave.

'This is very good,' she said after her first taste. Simple: grilled chicken and a warm pasta salad laced with a tomato, olive and basil sauce. Yet it tasted better than the food in most of the restaurants she ate at in London.

Will could've had a career as a chef, she mused. He didn't seem to have any cookery books around, so he clearly didn't make things from recipes. And yet he wasn't domesticated: it was just a question of being good at anything he tried. Will Daynes, she thought, was a bit like a wild flower. Sturdy, strong, and secure in his environment, but put him in the city and he'd droop. This was where he belonged. Not in her world.

'I love the huge skies out here,' he said. 'The way you can watch the sun set, and see the stars come out.'

'It's pretty,' she said, looking up at the clouds.

'A mackerel sky,' he said.

'Because it looks like the scales on a mackerel?' she guessed.

He nodded, looking pleased that she'd cottoned on so quickly. 'It means there's probably going to be some rain overnight.'

'The countryman's way of forecasting the weather?'

'Sure. Everyone knows the one about "red sky at night, shepherd's delight".' He gave her an easy smile. 'The saying that goes with this one is "mackerel sky, mackerel sky, never long wet and never long dry".'

'How do you *know* all this stuff?'

'Martin taught me some; and I read a lot as a kid.'

A sudden hardness in his expression warned her not to ask any more. She switched topic. 'Don't you find it lonely out here,' she asked, 'with these flat fields stretching out for miles and miles?'

'I couldn't live anywhere else but Cambridgeshire,' he said quietly. 'I like the empty spaces and wide skies.'

It was the opposite for her—she liked the busyness of London, where something was always happening, and although there were always people around they weren't endlessly inquisitive.

She and Will were complete opposites. And there could be no compromise. She couldn't settle out here; and he would never settle in London. They had no future together. So there was no point in starting something that would only end in tears.

She'd just have to keep her imagination on its usual tight rein.

CHAPTER EIGHT

TUESDAY STARTED off very similar to Monday—an early start and a drive to St John's Wood, but this time Sunny came with them and drowsed in a sunlit patch of grass while Will and Amanda worked on digging out the ground elder.

Despite her good intentions, Amanda couldn't stop thinking about the previous day and the way Will had kissed her. Worse, she couldn't stop wondering if he'd do it again...or suppress the disappointment when he didn't.

Halfway through the afternoon, Will's mobile phone rang. Although she tried not to listen to the conversation, she really couldn't help overhearing him. She was shocked to realise that he was talking figures. Prices and budgets and percentages. If she closed her eyes, she'd imagine she was listening to a man at a board meeting—a man wearing a dark suit, white shirt, silk tie and polished handmade shoes, with a set of figures and a laptop in front of him.

In real life, she was watching a man wearing faded, dusty jeans and an equally disreputable T-shirt, not to mention scruffy green wellies; instead of sitting on an executive chair in a board room, he was sprawled on a patch of grass and there weren't any papers in sight, let alone a computer.

And yet he was clearly more than holding his own in the conversation. All the necessary figures were in his head—did he have some kind of photographic memory? she wondered.

If it wasn't for the fact it was obvious that Will knew about plants, she'd think she'd been had. Because right now he didn't sound a bit like the hick countryman who was supposed to be her opposite. He sounded like a man well used to dealing with her world.

He wouldn't lie to her, though. She'd only known him a couple of days, but she was a good judge of character. Will Daynes wasn't the deceitful type.

She continued attacking the ground elder. Then something hot and clawlike raked over her arm. 'Ow!'

'You all right?' Will asked.

'Yes,' she fibbed.

But the soreness on her arm got worse. And when she looked at the painful area, she saw raised pink bumps all over it.

'Nettle rash,' Will said, taking a look at it. 'You got too close to the stingers. Sorry, I should've warned you to steer clear.'

She brushed it aside. 'I'll be okay.'

'Don't be such a martyr.' He pulled a leaf from a nearby plant. 'Here. Let me rub this over it.'

'Herbal medicine, now?' Embarrassment made her sharp.

'It's a dock leaf. Rub it on your arm and it'll stop the pain and swelling and make the rash go down quicker.' He shrugged and put the leaf back on the ground. 'Up to you if you prefer to be a victim and suffer.'

She grimaced, aware she'd been rude to him. 'Sorry. I didn't mean to snap. I'm just not used to people making a fuss over me.' She picked up the dock leaf and rubbed it against her skin. Strangely, her skin began to feel cooler almost immediately. 'Thanks for the advice.'

'No worries. Nettle stings aren't pleasant.' He gave her a sidelong look. 'Want to know something really weird about nettles?'

He had that mischievous little-boy look about him that she was beginning to find distinctly appealing. 'Go on.'

'They grow about thirty centimetres taller in land that has bodies buried in it—that's why they're always huge in churchyards.'

'How do you *know* this stuff?' she asked. Then, without giving him time to answer, said, 'Don't tell me—your uncle, Martin?'

'That's the one.'

'He sounds nice.'

'He is.'

And Will wasn't giving away any more information, she noted. He was even cagier about his background than she was. Strange.

Because surely parents would be proud of a son who was doing well in a job he loved?

Not that hers were proud of her. Her father was distant, and her mother… Well, she'd made no secret of the fact she resented the fact her daughter was doing what she hadn't been able to do. Even being a high flyer hadn't made Amanda fit into her family.

Sometimes, she wondered if she'd ever fit in anywhere. If she'd ever really belong.

She brushed the doubts away and continued digging. When she made partner, of course she'd belong. She'd have a place. And a car parking space with her name stamped all over it, to prove it.

Two sleepless nights hadn't done much for Will's equilibrium. Spending the Wednesday morning in the garden centre had made it worse, too. Sharing a desk—Martin's very untidy, messy desk—with Amanda, shuffling paperwork and looking at budgets and what-have-you. And all the time, he couldn't stop thinking about how he could sweep all the papers from it with one extravagant gesture, lift her on to the desktop and…

He was going crazy. There were dozens of reasons why he shouldn't do anything of the kind. Number one, there wasn't a lock on the door and anyone could walk in at any time and catch them in a very compromising position. Number two, Amanda had been wary of him since he'd kissed her among the ground elder on Monday afternoon, so giving in to the urge to grab her right now would make her even warier. Number three, it wasn't his desk anyway, and his dog happened to be sitting underneath it.

The list could go on and on and on.

And since when was a pair of bright green overalls a sexy garment anyway?

Since Amanda Neave had been wearing it, he thought grimly. He needed some fresh air to get some sense into his head again. Or, better still, caffeine.

'I need coffee,' he muttered. 'Want one?'

'Thanks. That'd be nice.' As he reached the door, she said his name.

He paused and looked back at her. 'What?'

'Are you all right?' she asked.

No. Because I can't stop thinking about kissing you, he thought. 'Sure,' he fibbed. 'Why?'

'You don't seem, um, in a very good mood today.'

'Lack of...' Sleep. Sex. '...caffeine.'

The coffee didn't help much, because he could still smell her perfume.

By lunchtime Will had had enough. If he didn't get out of here, right now, he knew he'd do something stupid. Like grabbing Amanda and kissing her until he forgot where he was.

'We're going into town,' he announced abruptly.

'Bunking off?' Amanda asked.

'No. Look, all the admin's been sorted. We've looked at stock figures and budgets.' He took a deep breath. 'And I can't do more than half a day in the office without going stir-crazy.'

'You're going to find next week a bit tough, then,' she observed.

'About as tough as you find it wearing jeans instead of a business suit,' he snapped back.

She raised an eyebrow. 'You really *are* out of sorts.'

'Sorry,' he muttered. 'I shouldn't take it out on you.'

'No offence taken.'

No. Because the cool, poised ice maiden didn't seem to get rattled about anything. She planned her way round everything. And Will felt an overwhelming need to see her melt. No, more than melt—he wanted to turn her into a volcano. He wanted to see her let go. He wanted to release the passion he was sure lay locked underneath that cool façade.

Right now.

'Let's go,' he announced.

He called over at the reception area on their way out to say that he was contactable on his mobile if anything cropped up, drove back to the cottage to drop Sunny home, then drove Amanda into Cambridge. With an effort, he remembered to leave the car in a car park rather than in the space outside his house, then marched her into a patisserie and ordered two baguettes.

'Ordering for me, now?' she asked.

He gave her a look that said very plainly, don't argue; it seemed to work, because she subsided. And she didn't say a word when he dragged her into another bakery for Chelsea buns. He needed a sugar fix.

He needed something much sweeter, actually. But a sugar fix would have to do.

For now.

'Chelsea buns?' she asked as they left the shop.

'World famous for them for the last eighty-odd years,' he said. 'They do the best chocolate cake in the world, too.'

And then, at last, they were in the Botanical Garden. He led Amanda over to the lakeside gardens and they sat down to eat their lunch, watching the birdlife and the dragonflies. Being in a garden usually soothed his soul, yet today the tension inside him wouldn't ease.

He lay back and closed his eyes. Right now he really needed his equilibrium back. He needed to get himself back under control.

And then he felt a hand stroke his hair back from his forehead.

Was he having some kind of physical hallucination, or had Amanda just…?

He opened his eyes to see her looking at him, her lower lip caught between her teeth.

'Amanda? Did you just…?' His voice faded at the embarrassment on her face—embarrassment, he guessed, at being caught acting completely out of character.

She flushed. 'Yes.'

'Why?'

She shook her head. 'I don't know. But I don't like it when you look sad. You're always smiling, always laid back. Today, you seem stressed. And I…' she sighed '…I don't know how to make you feel better. I'm not good at this sort of thing. I'm rubbish with people.'

Her eyes were a deep, intense blue—and filled with pain. Her words suddenly filtered into his consciousness. She felt bad because she didn't know how to make him smile…because she thought she wasn't good with people.

He sat up, curled his fingers round hers, and rubbed the pad of his thumb across the back of her hand. 'How do you mean, you're rubbish with people? You've been okay with me.'

She shook her head. 'I'm not like you, Will. People warm to you. They *like* you. You make their worlds light up. The staff at the garden centre, your customers, your clients—even when they're in a huff with you, you can still make them smile.' She looked bleak. 'Somehow, you seem to just charm them.'

He frowned. 'I don't set out to charm people.'

'You don't even have to try. It's inbuilt. I bet kids flock to you, and dogs and cats and…' Her voice actually sounded wobbly. She clearly knew it, because she closed her mouth and looked away from him.

'Hey.' He dropped her hand and put his arm round her, held her close. 'It's all right.'

She shrugged him away. 'Just ignore me. It must be PMT or something.'

No, it wasn't. She was being honest with him and letting him see a part of her she'd maybe never shown anyone else. And he wasn't going to let her hide it away again and bury the pain—like a splinter, it would fester and the feeling would get worse and worse. He took her hand again. 'You really think people don't like you?'

'I know they don't.' She didn't sound in the least bit self-pitying—typical Amanda, she was brisk and matter of fact about it. 'Even Dee…sometimes I think she just puts up with me because I don't give her any hassle, I'm never late paying my share of the rent and I don't leave the place in a mess like her last flatmate did.' When he continued to hold her, her words came out in a rush, as if they'd been walled up for years and years and years and finally the dam had burst. 'Her friends all think I'm too straight and boring. And even at work I don't really fit in. I bet you've never gone into work and heard people talking about a party at the weekend and then realised you were the only one who wasn't invited because you're not one of the crowd—you're not trendy or exciting to be with.'

His heart went out to her. She'd been rejected; and he'd just bet she'd done her best not to show how upset she was. The ice maiden, so cool and calm and collected. Except she was crying inside, where nobody could see.

'I'm sorry,' he said softly.

She lifted her chin in a clear attempt to be dismissive about it. 'I wouldn't have gone to the party anyway. I was busy.'

Working. That was obvious. 'But it still would've been nice to be invited.'

'I don't need pity. Not from you, not from anyone.' She took a deep breath. 'And if you tell anyone about this, I...I may just have to kill you.'

Brave words. A flip, throwaway phrase, an attempt at being funny—and it didn't work, because he could still hear the hurt in her voice. He stroked her face. 'I've got a better idea than that,' he said softly. 'Why don't you kiss me instead?'

Her eyes widened. 'What?'

'Kiss me,' he whispered. 'Let me kiss you back. Kiss you better.'

She shivered. 'We can't. We're in a public place.'

'Forty acres of garden. People come here to see the plants. They're not going to look at you and me. They're not going to notice one little kiss.' He scooped her up onto his lap to draw her closer. This was just where he wanted her. In his arms. 'If you'd been called Katharina instead of Amanda, I could've said, "Kiss me, Kate."'

Her eyes narrowed as she caught the reference. 'Are you saying I'm a shrew?'

He grinned. 'Ah, now I was banking on you not knowing your Shakespeare.' After all, she hadn't picked up on his reference to Cleopatra, in the punt.

'So now you think I'm ignorant.'

He saw the glimmer of hurt in her eyes before she masked it again, and he tightened his arms round her, not willing to let her wriggle off his lap. This was too important. 'No, I don't. But I do think maybe there's a valid point in this lifeswap stuff. Maybe we can teach each other things. Fill in the gaps for each other.' He leaned forward and kissed the tip of her nose. 'I don't think people *dislike* you, Amanda. I think they're scared of you. You have very exacting standards—and they're terrified they won't match up to them.' He paused. 'Do you really want to know why I was in a bad mood this morning?'

She was silent. Wide-eyed. And Lord, he wanted to kiss her. Kiss all the hurt away and make her smile again.

'I'll tell you anyway. It's because I kissed you on Monday. And I haven't been able to stop thinking about it since. In my head, I know this is crazy. You belong in a city, and I couldn't stand being in that sort of cage; just as you don't like the wide open spaces around here. But that's my head talking.' She'd told him a secret. He'd tell her one in return. Even up the balance. 'If I'd listened to my head, ten years ago, I probably would've ended up doing the same sort of job that you do.'

She blinked in surprise. 'You would've been an accountant?'

'Or worked in finance of some sort,' he agreed. 'I turned down an unconditional offer to read PPE at Oxford.'

'Why didn't you apply for botany or something instead?'

It wasn't the reaction he'd expected. He'd been sure that she would've sided with his parents, and claimed he was completely crazy for turning down the offer. But Amanda had seen the point straight away: it was the wrong course for him. And the way she'd asked why… It didn't sound judgemental. She really wanted to know his reasons for applying for the PPE.

'Because in my heart, I knew it wasn't what I wanted,' he said softly. 'I didn't want to work in a lab or in research, which is probably what would've happened if I'd chosen botany. I wanted to work with plants, with people. Garden design. Making magic. I only applied to Oxford to—well, to stop my parents nagging. I never had any intention of going there because they didn't do the course I wanted. Yes, if I'd listened to my head, I probably could've been earning ten times my current annual salary by now…but I would also have been seriously miserable. I'd probably have ended up drinking too much or doing recreational drugs to block out the fact I'd made the wrong choice.'

'Drugs?' She looked wary.

He smiled wryly, guessing what she wanted to know. 'Don't worry, I don't do them. Never have. I don't even drink that much— the occasional beer, a couple of glasses of wine if I'm out for dinner somewhere, and that's about all. What I'm trying to say— very badly—is that I had to make a choice. Listen to my heart or listen to my head. And I made the right choice for me. Not everyone agrees with that.' His parents still didn't. 'But sometimes less is more. And sometimes your head's plain wrong. Sometimes it's better to listen to your heart instead.' He took her hand and placed it on his heart. 'What does this say to you?'

'I don't know.'

'Then I'll translate it for you.' His gaze was fixed very firmly on her mouth. 'Kiss me.'

'I…I don't do this sort of thing. I don't have casual affairs.'

He had, in the past. But he had a nasty feeling there would be nothing casual about this. Which was yet another reason why he shouldn't do it. But he couldn't help smoothing the pad of his thumb over her lower lip. 'My head's telling me to stop right now. But my heart's telling me that this is right. Kiss me, Amanda.' He tilted his head back in invitation, wanting her to make the move.

Slowly, so slowly that he could barely hold his impatience in check, she reached up, slid her hands round his neck, and touched her mouth to his. Almost shyly, at first—a kiss so sweet that it made his bones melt.

Even though he wanted to pull her closer, deepen the kiss and let this thing between them explode, he let her set the pace. It was a lovely gentle kiss that made him ache for more.

She pulled back, and he saw a single tear trickle down her cheek.

'Ah, honey. Don't cry.' He kissed the tear away. 'I'm not going to pressure you.'

'This isn't supposed to happen. It's meant to be business. You're messy and disorganised and—'

'And you're a control freak who's neat and tidy and has always got one eye on the clock. Let's throw away the rules and see what happens.' He stroked her hair away from her face. 'Just so you know…I'm not going to sign a confidentiality thing about what you told me.'

He saw the faintest, faintest hint of fear in her eyes.

'Because,' he continued, 'I want you to trust me. You don't *need* me to sign anything because I'm not going to tell anyone. It's just between you and me. Just as I know you're not going to tell anyone what I told you. And even though there's nothing I want more right now than to carry you home to my bed and make love with you until we're both dizzy, we're going to stand up and stroll through the gardens and look at structure and form and colour. Light and shade. I want you, Amanda, but I'm not going to push you.'

'No?'

He smiled. 'That's the thing about gardening. You learn to be patient. Wait until the time's right.' Gently, he lifted her off his lap. Stood up. Helped her to her feet. And refused to let her hand go.

'I thought you said you were patient?' she whispered.

He raised her hand to his mouth and kissed the backs of her fingers. 'To a degree. I'm not setting any time limits.' He kept his fingers twined through hers and began to walk through the gardens. 'To get your perfect bloom, you need to be patient. But you also need to be persistent. That's something I'm very, very good at.' He slanted her an intense look. 'And that, honey, is a promise.'

CHAPTER NINE

WILL KEPT his word. He didn't push Amanda; he didn't even try to kiss her again, that night. But over dinner, when he was talking about work and gardens, she could see in his eyes that he was thinking about kissing her, and remembering the heat that had flared between them that afternoon. The thought made her whole body tingle with anticipation.

There's nothing I want more right now than to carry you home to my bed.

Will the pirate, sweeping her off her feet.

Let's throw away the rules.

She wanted to. How she wanted to. But if she threw away the rules, and threw away the structure she'd built round her life...Fear seeped through her. What then? What if she fell so hard for Will that she'd never bounce back again when it was over?

Because it wouldn't last. It couldn't last. He'd said it himself. *You belong in a city, and I couldn't stand being in that sort of cage; just as you don't like the wide open spaces.*

There was no possible compromise.

Sometimes it's better to listen to your heart instead...my heart's telling me that this is right.

But supposing his heart was wrong?

She dared not take that risk.

On Thursday, too, he kept things light; they spent an hour at the garden centre, sorting out some admin, and then went to see another of Will's clients for an initial discussion. She filmed him and listened, fascinated, as Will skilfully drew out what the client really wanted from the space. How did he do that? How did he get people to open up to him in that way?

'And now it's the technical stuff,' he said with a smile. 'You'll like this, Amanda. It's structured.'

That stung. Did he really think she was so buttoned up?

Well. He was right. She *was*.

She pushed the hurt aside. 'So this might be good to film.'

'If you like. But you're going to do some of this with me. First, we'll test the soil type.'

'Chemicals?' she guessed.

'One of the tests involves a pH indicator, yes.' He fetched a cardboard box from the back of his car. 'Right. First we need a soil sample.' He took a metal pole with a pointed end from the box, took samples, then put a handful of soil into a glass jar which he filled with water and stirred.

'That's for the pH thing?' she asked.

'No, this is sediment so we can see the type. This one's the pH—different plants like different levels of acidity or alkalinity, though my gut feeling is that this is going to be neutral.'

'How do you know?'

'Take a handful of the sample and look at it,' he advised.

She did. 'And?'

'How does it feel?'

'Sticky.' Enlightenment dawned. 'It's clay?'

'We'll see from the sediment test—but I'd say so.' He added another sample to a small test tube that contained powder, added some water, put a stopper on the top and shook it up before placing it in a rack.

'Right—while those are settling we'll do the measurements.' He took another gadget from the box.

'What's that?'

'My new toy—an electronic measure. Obviously, it only works if there's a solid structure to bounce the rays off; if there isn't, it's back to a good old-fashioned tape measure.' He gave her a sidelong look and drawled, 'Want to play with me?'

She knew he was teasing her. But her body responded anyway, a tingling surge of desire starting at the base of her spine that ran right down to the ends of her fingers and toes. 'Boys and their toys,' she said sniffily.

His eyes went gold with mischief. 'I could *dare* you to play with me.'

So tempting. What would he do if she called his bluff and kissed him? Wrapped her arms round his neck, pressed her body close to his and nibbled his lower lip? Would he open his mouth, let her deepen the kiss? Would he take control? Would he incite her to take charge?

She folded her arms to stop herself acting on the urge. 'We have work to do.'

He smiled, but Amanda marvelled at the ease with which he switched from playfulness to seriousness, taking the measurements and noting them meticulously.

Then he took photographs.

She frowned. 'The files you gave me showed sketches. Going into the modern age now, are we?' she asked.

He laughed. 'No. I'll do the sketches later. This is an *aide-mémoire*—quicker than a sketch.' There was the most appealing dimple in his cheek as he added, 'Neater, too. Right—aspect, next.'

'And you test that how?'

'Sitting in a deckchair for the day with a long, cold drink and a good book.'

She blinked. 'You're joking.'

'Spend a day lazing around a garden and you can really see how the light changes,' he said. 'Though as we're doing this *efficiently*…' He produced another gadget from his box. 'It's west-facing.'

She was surprised that he actually needed to use a compass to tell that. Will probably knew how to navigate by starlight.

She tried to ignore the idea of being under the stars in Will's company. Just the two of them and a million pinpoints of light. 'West-facing's good?' she asked.

'South-facing's the best aspect for a garden,' he said, 'but this still gets a lot of light—afternoon and evening sun rather than morning.' He walked over to the jar and test tube. 'You see this water's cloudy and there's only a little bit of sediment at the bottom?'

It had been years since she'd done any chemistry or biology. 'Yes. Because you haven't left it long enough?'

'It'll still be like this in an hour, because this is clay soil and the particles take ages to settle. It confirms what you said: clay.

Which usually means neutral pH, so we can grow virtually anything there—we could add a bit of lime to make it more alkaline, but if our client likes acid-loving plants we'll have to think about making a raised bed with different soil, or container gardening.'

We. Except her time shadowing him was almost over. When the lifeswap project had finished, she wouldn't see him again. She wouldn't see what he planned for the garden here; wouldn't see the actress's garden turn from the sketch on the page into the living colour of Will's vision; wouldn't see the rose arbour replacing all that ground elder in the footballer's garden.

And she was shocked by how sad that made her feel.

She shook the feeling aside and asked coolly, 'So what does the chemical test tell you?'

'It's bright green. That means neutral,' Will said. 'So that's fine. The client's going to do me a mood board over the next couple of weeks, and we can take it from there.'

'We' again. But there was no 'we'. No 'us', she thought.

They called in to a supermarket on the way home—at least, Will did. He informed her that she was staying put. Clearly he planned to cook her something nice as a surprise, as this was her last evening here. Still, at least it meant she could check her emails on her mobile phone and see how her team was getting on with the audit. On Saturday she'd be back in the office and could look over the files for herself.

'Tut. Sneaking in some of your own work. Is this allowed under the lifeswap rules?' a voice whispered in her ear.

She'd been concentrating so hard, she hadn't realised Will was back; his voice made her jump. 'Oh! Yes. Of course it is,' she said crossly, flicking out of the emails and turning off the phone. 'Look, you're going to want to check that things are going smoothly at the garden centre next week, aren't you?'

He didn't reply, just gave her a wry look, which she interpreted as meaning no.

He didn't let her help unpack things from the car, either—just shooed her upstairs to have a bath. 'And don't put your business suit on,' he added. 'No armour required, okay?'

On the contrary. Where Will Daynes was concerned, she

needed all the armour she could get. But she did as he requested and wore the faded denims he'd bought her. Though, just to prove she wasn't a doormat, bowing to his every command, she wore a shirt rather than a T-shirt, rolling the sleeves up to her elbows.

When she returned downstairs, Will barred her way to the kitchen and handed her a glass of wine. 'Go and chill out in the garden.'

'Look, I know cooking's not my thing, but don't you want me to set the table or something?'

'Remember what we were saying earlier this week about the senses?'

Trust him to answer a question with a question. She sighed. 'Yes.'

'Indulge me,' he said, 'because I'm going to teach you about the importance of taste.'

She felt her eyes narrow. 'Does this have anything to do with the fact that I don't cook?'

He gave her the most mischievous grin. 'That might have a bit of a bearing on it, yes. I'm not sure I can cope with a week of pre-packaged food.'

She frowned. 'It's perfectly nutritious. You're making a fuss over nothing.'

'Am I?' His eyes glittered. 'Tell me that in a few minutes. Now off you go. If you see what I'm preparing, it's going to defeat the object.'

'Surely I'll smell dinner?'

He handed her a glass of wine. 'Not necessarily. Indulge me, Amanda. Go and sit outside in the garden.'

A few minutes later, he walked outside. 'Ready?'

She nodded.

'No, don't get up. We're going to eat out here tonight.' He smiled at her. 'Close your eyes.'

'Why?'

He sighed. 'Maybe I should make you wear a blindfold for this.'

A blindfold? Her cheeks scorched as a decadent image slid into her mind. Herself, naked except for a blindfold, lying back against silk sheets in a pirate's boudoir, and Will the pirate locking the door behind them so they wouldn't be disturbed...

That wine really must have gone to her head.

'Just close your eyes, Amanda. And no peeking.'

'Okay,' she whispered.

She heard the noise of something being placed on the cast-iron table—a plate or tray of some sort, she guessed.

'Keep your eyes closed,' Will reminded her. 'And trust me. Agreed?'

'Agreed.'

'Good.'

She felt something sliding against her lower lip.

'Eyes closed,' he insisted, just as she was about to open them. 'Tell me. How does it feel?'

'Cold. Smooth.'

'Open your mouth,' he said softly, and slid the morsel inside. 'Now eat it. Then describe it to me.'

She recognised the taste instantly. 'An olive.'

'And it tastes of?'

'Olive.'

He groaned. 'That olive was marinated in chilli and thyme, I'll have you know. Okay, so your sense of taste needs a bit of fine-tuning. Next.'

'Cool. Wet. Slippery.' Again, the taste was recognisable. 'A chunk of cucumber.'

'And this?'

'Soft.' She heard the murmur of frustration before he managed to mute it. Okay, she'd try and give him what he wanted. 'It's sweet and salty and a bit tart, all at the same time. It's obviously cheese, but I'm not sure which type.'

'Feta.'

'You're feeding me a Greek salad?' she guessed.

He laughed. 'No fooling you, is there? So what's missing?'

'Tomato?'

'Uh-huh. This time, I want you to describe the scent.'

She breathed in. 'It smells of…tomato.'

'This is a baby plum tomato off the vine. It smells gorgeous, like a greenhouse on a hot summer day.' He groaned. 'Don't you *ever* do flowery language?'

'You mean, like these wine buffs who talk about a hint of gooseberry and new-mown grass?'

He laughed. 'I think that's a perfect description of the sauvignon blanc you've just been drinking.' He fed her more bites of salad. 'Right. Scent again.'

She shook her head. 'Don't know this one.'

'What does it conjure up?'

'Something woody. A hillside in Greece.'

'Hallelujah. Finally she gets it.' He rubbed the morsel against her lips and her mouth parted.

'Mmm. Bread. A bit salty. And something else—a taste I don't know.'

'Rosemary bread. It's best warm, dipped in olive oil.'

'Can I open my eyes now and just eat this normally?'

'No. I'm enjoying myself.' He fed her delicate morsels of lemon-scented chicken, more bread and more Greek salad.

'I'm starting to feel a bit stupid,' she said, wriggling in her seat.

'You don't look it. But okay, this is the last one. I want a proper description. How does this feel?'

'Bumpy. Shiny—no, wait, something can't feel shiny, can it?'

'Shiny's fine.' There was laughter in his voice, but she knew he was laughing with her, not at her. 'Take a bite.'

It was the sweetest, juiciest strawberry she'd ever eaten—and she could feel a tiny rivulet of juice running down from the corner of her mouth. She was about to lick it away—but then Will beat her to it.

She opened her eyes. 'Will!'

'Hey. There's only so much temptation a man can stand.' He brushed his mouth against hers. 'You taste of strawberries. And I'm *hungry*, Amanda.'

'Then you should have eaten properly instead of feeding me like a baby,' she said, striving to sound cool and collected and the complete opposite of how she felt right now, gazing into the sexiest eyes she'd ever seen and so very close to the sexiest mouth that had ever taken hers.

'I wasn't feeding you like a baby, honey. I was feeding you like a lover,' he told her huskily.

Oh-h-h. Desire trickled between her shoulderblades.

One more kiss and she knew she'd say yes. This had to stop. 'This isn't a good idea, Will.'

'No?'

'We're too different. You don't belong in London, and I don't belong here.'

'We're more similar than you think,' he said softly. 'And it's not a question of *belonging*. I don't know where this is going to take us. I don't even know what I'm offering you. There's just something about you that tips me off balance.'

Yeah. She knew that feeling.

'When we were in Grantchester Meadows, and you were looking up at the sky, all soft and sweet with your face full of wonder as you really heard birdsong for the first time…I wanted to kiss you then.'

She'd wanted him to kiss her, too.

'And yesterday, in the Botanical Garden…' He pressed a kiss into her palm and folded her fingers over it. 'I want to kiss you now.' The lightest brush of his lips against the pulse beating in her wrist. 'I love how soft your skin is.' A trail of tiny butterfly kisses up to her inner elbow. 'How sweet you smell.' He nuzzled the sensitive spot in the curve of her neck. 'How sweet you taste,' he whispered.

She was nearly hyperventilating. Lord, his voice was so sexy. And the feel of his mouth against her skin was driving her wild.

'I want to kiss you, Amanda. Right here, right now.'

That was it. She closed her eyes again and tipped her head back, offering him her throat.

'But even more than that…' he took the tiniest, gentlest, *sexiest* bite, just grazing his teeth against her skin, and she shuddered with need '…even more than that, I want you to kiss me back. Let go. Let go the way you didn't yesterday. Turn me to flames.'

She slid her hands into his hair, and nibbled at his lower lip; he opened his mouth, letting her deepen the kiss, and it suddenly became hot and wet and wild.

She wasn't aware of their mouths ever leaving each other's, but they must have done at some point because now her hands were gliding over bare skin and hard, well-defined muscles. Will's shoulders. Somehow, she must have stripped off his T-shirt. She couldn't even remember doing it.

And she was no longer buttoned up. He'd undone every single button on her shirt. Untucked the soft cotton from the waistband of her jeans. And he was nuzzling the vee between her breasts, slowly pulling the edge of her bra down to expose her nipples. The contrast between his dark hair and her fair skin sent a jolt through her.

And oh, Lord, as his mouth closed over one hard peak, she whimpered, 'Will!'

He lifted his head, his molten-silver gaze matching hers. 'What?'

'We—we can't do this. We're outside. In the garden.' Her breath hitched. 'Anyone can see us.'

'Not here,' he reassured her softly. 'We're at the back of the house. There's nobody in the fields. Just you and me and the wide open skies. But if you'd rather…' He got to his feet and scooped her up so she was forced to cling round his neck for balance. Her naked breasts rubbed against the hair on his naked chest and she'd never been so turned on in her entire life. 'I'll carry you indoors.' He punctuated each word with a kiss. 'To. My. Bed.'

The last vestiges of her common sense roared in her ears. 'Will—no.'

He froze. Then, with what was clearly a huge effort, he lowered her until her feet touched the floor, then restored order to her clothes. As he did up every single button, his fingers brushed against her skin; and his eyes were telling her that she could change her mind at any time. All she had to do was say 'yes'.

And she wanted to. How she wanted to.

But her head wouldn't let her make that kind of mistake.

Her legs still felt so weak, she needed to hold on to the chair for support. 'I'm sorry,' she whispered.

His face was completely unreadable. 'I'm not going to force you, Amanda. I'd never do that.' He dragged in a breath. 'But I warn you now, this thing between us isn't going away any time soon.'

She shook her head. 'It can't work between us.'

'You don't know that. Neither do I. We could be brave, give it a try. See where this takes us.'

Brave. That was the point. She was too scared. Too scared that she'd lose her heart to him and then he'd be like everyone else, deciding that her face didn't fit and she'd be left…empty. 'I can't,' she whispered. 'I just *can't.*'

He looked at her for a long, long moment. As if he were battling with himself, fighting the urge to ignore what she'd said and carry her off like a pirate. She saw a muscle tighten in his jaw.

And then he nodded. 'I'll respect your wishes.' He pulled his T-shirt on. 'I'll take Sunny for a walk to give us some breathing space.'

Enough to restore her equilibrium. His, too.

How she wished it could've been different. But it wouldn't work. It *couldn't* work. She needed to listen to her head. Even though her heart was telling her to grab him before he walked away, kiss him until they were both crazy with need, and just let it happen—she needed to listen to her head. Cool, calm, common sense. Keep things strictly business between them.

CHAPTER TEN

WILL WAS gone for an hour. And from the way he walked into the kitchen with damp, curly hair and Sunny drained a whole bowl of water before curling up on her bed, Amanda guessed that he'd been for a run rather than a walk to get rid of his frustration.

Frustration that she'd caused by calling a halt, when they were already half-naked. She'd led him on and made him stop. Guilt flickered through her. 'Will. I'm sorry,' she said again.

'Not a problem.' He shrugged. 'We'll both pretend it didn't happen.'

'Thanks.'

Though it was easier said than done. A lot, lot easier. She slept incredibly badly that night. Half a dozen times, she thought about climbing out of the double bed and knocking on Will's door. Saying yes.

Common sense stopped her. Just.

But the next morning, her eyes felt heavy and her head ached.

A hot shower didn't make her feel any better. In fact, she couldn't remember the last time she'd felt this miserable. This empty.

She should've said yes.

Even if it had been a one-night stand, it would've been worth it. Too late, now.

'Morning,' Will said when she walked into the kitchen.

He didn't look too brilliant, either. There were dark smudges under his eyes, as if he'd slept as badly as she had last night.

'Morning,' she muttered.

He pushed a mug of coffee over to her, and topped up his own. 'So. Last day of you shadowing me.'

'Uh-huh.'

'Have you enjoyed your week in the country?' he asked.

Making polite conversation. Well. She could be equally polite. 'More than I expected to.'

'Good.' He looked at her, and for a moment that hungry pirate look was back. 'Will you have dinner with me before you go tonight?'

She shook her head. 'I need to get back to London. And you'll be busy catching up with whatever you need to sort out for next week.'

Was it his imagination, or had her cheeks turned very slightly pink? Was she scared that they'd take up where they'd left off last night—and that this time he wouldn't stop if she tried to call a halt?

Ah, hell. This mess was all his fault. He shouldn't have pushed her, last night. But the way her even white teeth had sunk into the strawberry, the way her beautiful mouth had smiled at him…he just hadn't been able to resist kissing her. Letting the heat rise between them.

'Yeah, you're right. I have things to do.' Such as getting the holiday cottage back to how it was supposed to be, then sorting his house out. He just hoped that his neighbour had remembered her promise to water his plants and he wasn't going to return to utter carnage on his patio.

'Um…there's one thing. About Sunny. When I agreed to do this lifeswap thing, I didn't realise you had a dog. And—well—my rental agreement says no pets,' she said.

'Not a problem. Fliss is looking after her for the week.' He smiled at her, pleased that she'd been worried about the dog. 'I imagine you have to catch the tube to work, and as dogs aren't allowed unless they're guide dogs, it'd mean leaving her in a strange place, which wouldn't be fair. At least she knows Fliss.'

They spent the rest of the day at the house in St John's Wood, tackling the ground elder again. Then there was lunch at a pub followed by more ground elder. And finally he drove them back to the Fens. The last time.

The music he was playing seemed to be giving her some sort of message—slow country-rock ballads with promises that the singer would be there for her, love her more than she'd ever been loved, that the future would be fine because they were together.

When he began to sing along with the music—and Lord, he had a gorgeous voice—she was even more sure that he was trying to tell her something.

But then her common sense kicked in. Will couldn't possibly give her promises like that. He was just singing along to songs he liked and had played often enough to know the words and the melody.

Back at the cottage, she packed her things swiftly. And saying goodbye to Will was awkward. 'Thanks for, um, teaching me about gardens,' she mumbled.

'Pleasure.' He was equally polite and formal. 'I'll see you on Sunday evening, then. And you can teach me…'

What? What the hell could she teach Will, whose life was chaotic, but it didn't matter because he was happy that way? How to be buttoned-up and avoid people?

Not in a million years.

She wished she'd suggested taking her car to St John's Wood as well, so she could've said goodbye to him at the garden, where it would've been quick and relatively painless. But she'd been too sleep-deprived this morning to think straight. 'See you Sunday,' she said, avoiding his eyes, and made her escape.

Will leaned against the doorjamb, watching Amanda drive away. Now there would be two days of space between them. More than enough time for her to rebuild every single wall. And next week he'd be in her world, on her schedule.

The kind of life his parents had planned for him.

The kind of life he'd promised himself he'd never have to lead.

Somehow he didn't think he'd last the week without breaking a few rules.

'Let's get this place tidy,' he told Sunny, 'and then we're going home.'

'So, how was it?' Dee asked.

Amanda shrugged. 'Fine.'

'Are you sure?' Dee looked worried. 'You've hardly said a

word since you've been home. You had an early night last night—a *really* early night.'

'That's what all that fresh air and digging gardens does for you,' Amanda said.

'Well, you don't look rosy-cheeked and bushy-tailed or however you're supposed to look after a week in the country.'

She didn't feel it, either. 'Probably because I'm a city girl and smelling the roses gets pretty boring after a while.'

Dee bit her lip. 'Sorry. Was it really awful?'

Yes. Because I think I might have fallen in love with someone who's so wrong for me, it's untrue. And because I can't stop thinking about him. And because I think I might have made a huge mistake in saying no. And because I know that saying yes would be an even bigger mistake. 'It was okay,' Amanda lied. 'I'm not sure what I can teach him, though.'

Dee coughed. 'Yeah. He pretty much makes his own decisions.'

'How well do you know him?' Amanda asked.

'Um…well, as you probably know by now, he's Fliss's brother. So I've known him since he was a spotty, gangly sixteen-year-old.' Dee smiled wryly. 'If anyone had told me then he'd turn out to be six foot two of gorgeous man, I'd have said they were mad. He was just Fliss's annoying kid brother back then. Actually, he's a lovely guy. He's got a big heart. But he has his own ideas about things. And he can be a bit stubborn.'

'I noticed.'

'Ouch.' Dee flinched. 'Look, you can call off this second week if you really hated each other that much.'

That was just the problem, Amanda thought. They hadn't hated each other. Far from it. 'I said I'd do this. I'm not going to let you down.'

She just hoped she wouldn't let herself down, either—by falling at Will Daynes's feet the second he walked into her flat.

'Rightio—you're off to Aunty Fliss's for the week,' Will informed Sunny.

The dog looked at the car, and then at Will as if to say, 'Please, can't we just stay here?'

He knew how she felt. The second he'd opened the door, she'd searched the entire house, sniffing every nook and cranny to make sure her home was still there exactly as she'd left it. And he'd made a beeline for the kitchen-cum-conservatory, his favourite place. It had been built to his specifications, so the glass addition complemented the Victorian terrace: the place where his garden and his house merged.

The plants on his patio were still lush and green, to his relief; his neighbour had more than deserved the flowers and chocolates he'd picked up on his way home to say thank you. And then he'd had dinner on his own. A meal where he'd just gone through the motions of cooking and fed half of it to Sunny because he wasn't in the mood for eating: and he was shocked to realise that he actually missed Amanda.

How could she have got so deeply under his skin in six days?

And although he hated the idea of leaving home again so quickly, it wasn't so bad—even though he'd be in London—because he'd be with *her*.

'Oh, no. Please tell me you haven't,' Fliss said, the second she opened the front door to him.

'What?'

'You've got a moony look on your face. Please tell me you haven't fallen for the Ice Queen.'

Will frowned. 'She's not icy.'

Fliss sighed. 'Amanda Neave is about the worst possible woman you could fall for. Her career comes first, last and all the spaces in between—and I don't want to see you get hurt.'

The way he'd been hurt by their parents, who'd done exactly the same thing. 'I'm not going to get hurt.' Will folded his arms. 'And may I remind you that you asked me to do this lifeswap thing in the first place?'

'I know. And I'm beginning to wish I hadn't.' Fliss bit her lip. 'I really didn't think she'd be your type.'

'I don't *have* a type,' he said. 'I'm not that shallow. And this really isn't a problem.'

'Hmm.' Fliss clearly wasn't convinced, because she fussed over him during lunch. To the point where he ended up shepherding her into the kitchen and made her sit down.

'Right. Let's take this step by step. The age at which you're of-ficially an adult—when you can drive and own a house and vote and get married without parental consent—is…?'

'Eighteen.'

'And my age is…?'

She sighed. 'Twenty-nine.'

'So logically, I've been an adult for…? Come on, Fliss, even you can do the maths,' he added with a teasing grin.

She glared at him. 'Eleven years. But you're still my baby brother.'

'And you really don't need to worry about me. Look at me, Fliss. I'm together and I'm happy. I have my own house and I have a job—my own business, if we're being pernickety, and it's doing fine. I don't do drugs and I stay on the right side of the law—well, apart from those two speeding tickets eight years ago, and I learned my lesson very quickly. I don't repeat my mistakes.'

Fliss reached out and ruffled his hair. 'I know. But I just don't want to see you get a broken heart from falling in love with someone who wouldn't be good for you.'

'I'm not in love with Amanda.' He was more than halfway there, but he was trying to be sensible about it. 'And even if I was, you don't know for definite that she'd be bad for me. Trust me to be the judge of that, hmm?' He smiled to take the edge from his words. 'You know, I'll be very, very glad when my niece or nephew appears and you can stop practising your parenting skills on me.'

Fliss's eyes filled with tears. 'I don't mean to be bossy. It's just…I love you.'

'And I love you, too, sis.' He gave her a hug. 'Now, stop worry-ing about me. I'm old enough and big enough to take care of myself. If I had a problem, you'd be the first one I'd come to. Okay?'

She nodded.

With the pad of his thumb, he brushed away the tear sliding down her cheek. 'Please stop crying, or Cal will have my guts for garters for upsetting his pregnant wife.'

'It's just hormones,' she sniffed.

On cue, Cal walked in, took one look at his wife and groaned. 'Oh, no. What did you do, Will? Tell her you loved her, or some-thing?'

'Yeah.' Will wrinkled his nose. 'It was meant to stop her nagging. She was being bossy.'

'Part of the job description for a schoolmarm,' Cal teased, walking over to his wife and kissing her.

'I'd better ring for a taxi,' Will said, 'or I'll miss my train to London.'

'I'll drive you in to town,' Cal said. 'And you, honey, need to put your feet up in the meantime and *rest*,' he reminded his wife.

Fliss groaned. 'I'm perfectly all right, Cal.'

Will laughed. 'Dosed with your own medicine, sis.' He dropped to a crouch and made a fuss of Sunny. 'Look after her and make sure she behaves herself, okay?' He looked up at his sister. 'And I'm talking to her, not you. I know my dog'll be on her best behaviour.'

'Oh, *you*,' Fliss said, rolling her eyes.

But at least she was smiling again, he thought. 'See you when I get back from London.' He hugged his sister goodbye. 'And thanks for looking after Sunny for me.'

'It's the least I could do, considering I lumbered you with this in the first place.'

When Cal had dropped him in the city centre, Will headed for a certain florist he knew, then caught the train to London. Two changes of Tube lines later and he was at the road leading to Amanda's flat.

This was it. He took a deep breath and rang the intercom.

A few moments later, he heard her say, 'Hello?'

The weird jolt in the region of his heart was unsettling. How could just the sound of her voice do that to him? He pulled himself together. 'Hi. It's Will.'

'Come up.'

He heard the buzzer go and pushed the door open.

Just as he'd expected, she was back in a business suit. The buttoned-up finance whiz, not the woman who'd started to turn to fire in his arms.

'Hello,' he said.

She didn't meet his eyes. 'I'll just get you a permit for your car, so you don't get a parking ticket.'

'No need. I know parking's at a premium in London, so I came by Tube.'

That made her look at him. 'So how are you going to get home?'

'Taxi from Cambridge train station.' Although he lived within walking distance of the train station, he'd left his car at Fliss's. 'Oh—these are for you.' He brought his hands from behind his back and gave her the flowers.

She stared at him, looking shocked; clearly she didn't receive flowers very often, he thought. 'You didn't need to do that,' she said; then recovered swiftly. 'Thank you. It's very kind.'

So cool and polite. He wanted the woman who'd kissed him back. Though it looked as if she was in hiding—and it was going to take a while to tempt her out.

He'd bought her flowers. Cool, elegant calla lilies. A huge sheaf of them, arranged professionally, and they must've cost him a small fortune. When had someone last given her flowers—let alone flowers that had been chosen personally?

'I'll put these in water, then show you to your room,' she said.

Over the last two days, she'd managed to gloss over the way he made her feel, almost to the point where she thought she could treat him like any other male of her acquaintance, a colleague or client. But now he was in her space and she realised how wrong she was.

Will Daynes simply radiated energy.

And sex.

And there was no way she was going to get any sleep tonight, knowing that his bed was only a few feet away from her own.

He'd followed her into the kitchen so she arranged the flowers carefully, not wanting Will to know how much it rattled her that he'd closed the space between them. 'Dee's away at a conference for the week, so you'll be staying in her room.' Without meeting his gaze, she showed him round the flat. 'Living room—well, obviously. Bathroom. Your room. I've put a fresh towel on the bed, but there are more in the airing cupboard.'

'Thank you.'

She eyed his suitcase. It didn't look that big. Then she looked at Will again. He was wearing faded jeans, a clean but old T-shirt, and trainers. No way could she take him into the office like this.

'You're not planning on going to the office dressed like that, are you?' she asked.

He gave her a lazy smile that made ripples of lust lick down her spine. 'What do you think?'

Oh, Lord. He *was*. Lust turned to dread. 'Will, it's Sunday evening and no shops are open!' She dragged in a breath. 'Okay. We'll just have to go in late tomorrow. We'll go in via Oxford Street and get you a suit on the way to the office.'

His smile broadened. 'You're panicking, aren't you?'

'Are you surprised? Look, you knew exactly what we were doing this week. I gave you a schedule. I thought you'd—'

'Dress appropriately?' he cut in, his eyes sparkling.

Then she realised that he was teasing her. 'That's unkind,' she said, glaring at him.

'I'm sorry. But you were being stuffy. I couldn't resist it.' He smiled at her. 'I'm not going to show you up, Amanda. I do own a suit. Though I'll probably need to borrow your iron tomorrow morning to get the creases out of my shirt.'

The thought of Will, bare-chested, ironing a shirt, made her heart miss a beat. It had been three days, and she still remembered exactly what his naked chest had looked like. Still remembered how his skin had felt against hers. Still—

Oh, she really had to get a grip. 'Can I get you a drink, while you put your things away?' she asked.

'Something cold would be lovely, thanks. Whatever you've got.'

For a moment, she thought he was going to reach out and touch her; she tensed, but then the moment was gone and he picked up his suitcase. 'See you in a minute.'

A whole evening. How on earth was she going to spend a *whole evening* with him? She almost cut herself when she sliced the lemon, because she wasn't paying attention to what she was doing—she was remembering the feel of Will's mouth against hers.

Well, this time she'd exercise some self-control. Five days, that was all—they'd agreed it would end on Friday afternoon at three. She could keep some distance between them for five days, surely?

But when she returned to the living room and handed Will his glass, her fingers brushed against his. It felt like pure electricity fizzing through her veins. It was the same for him, too; she could tell by the way his pupils dilated and his eyes changed colour from serious green to that sexy molten silver.

'What time do we leave for the office tomorrow?' he asked.

'I usually leave here at seven,' she said.

He sighed. 'I had a feeling it was going to be something like that.'

'Except on Wednesdays, when I leave at six and have an hour in the gym first.'

'And I have to go to the gym, too?'

She nodded. 'It's all part of the shadowing, isn't it?'

He raised an eyebrow. 'I can't remember when I last set foot in a gym. Oh, well.'

'I'm sure you won't have any problems. Your muscles are...' Her mouth dried.

'My muscles are?' he prompted.

'Never mind.'

'Too big? Too small?' He paused and said huskily, 'Just right?'

Oh, yes. They were just right. She dragged in a breath. 'You're used to physical exercise. From gardening, I mean, and taking Sunny for a walk.'

His mouth quirked. 'You're blushing, Amanda.'

'No, I'm not.' She folded her arms. Come on, come on—surely she could think of something neutral to say? She fell back on the old standby. 'So your degree was in horticulture. Which A-levels did you do?'

He smiled, as if knowing exactly why she'd asked. To keep the conversation cerebral instead of sensual. 'Maths, economics, biology and chemistry.'

She frowned. She'd expected the economics—after all, he'd applied to read PPE at Oxford—but she'd thought he'd studied English. 'How come you know so much Shakespeare and poetry, then?'

'I used to go out with an actress. I helped her learn her lines by reading the other parts for her. I think my favourite's *Antony and Cleopatra*. Sheer poetry. "Eternity was in our lips and eyes..."' He drew the tip of his tongue against his lower lip, and she couldn't help watching him, fascinated. 'Funny how I can't stop thinking of mouths when I'm with you,' he added softly.

'That's not fair. This is meant to be business.'

'Then I'll do you a deal.' His eyes glittered. 'Kiss me, and I'll shut up.'

She remembered the last time they'd kissed. They'd both become so carried away, they'd ended up being half-naked. Outside. Completely oblivious to everything and everyone. 'No deal.'

He grinned. 'So I don't have to shut up? Good.'

'That isn't what I meant, and you know it.'

'Are you afraid to kiss me?' he taunted.

'No.' *Yes.*

His smile vanished and he looked serious. 'For what it's worth, what happened on Thursday—that doesn't normally happen to me. I never forget where or who I am. And I don't think you do, either.'

'No,' she admitted. And she really hoped he hadn't heard that wobble in her voice. The shiver of pure desire.

'I can't stop thinking about it,' he said softly.

Neither could she. 'Well, you'll just have to,' she said, trying to sound as prim and proper as she could. 'It's not part of the lifeswap thing.'

'No.' But his eyes were saying something completely different.

It's going to happen.

Soon.

And neither of us will want to stop.

CHAPTER ELEVEN

AMANDA'S HAND was on the door to the bathroom when it opened abruptly and she almost pitched forward straight into Will, who was wearing nothing but a towel slung low over his hips, and his hair was still damp.

'Sorry,' she muttered. 'I didn't realise you were…'

Since when had she lost her ability to form a sentence?

She was really, really glad that her dressing gown was thick towelling—she'd be mortified if he could see how just the sight of his half-naked body had turned her on. With difficulty, she pulled herself together. 'I've left the iron and ironing board out for you in the living room.'

'Thanks.'

She showered and washed her hair; but she couldn't get the thought out of her head that, just a few moments before, Will's naked body had been in exactly the same place hers was right now. What would it be like to share a shower with—?

Don't even *think* about it, she warned herself.

But her head wasn't listening. It was creating pictures of Will ironing his shirt, naked to the waist, the muscles on his back flexing. And by the time she'd finished dressing and went into the kitchen to make breakfast, she was quivering.

'I made you some coffee,' he said, and handed her a mug.

'Thanks.' Please, please let the caffeine jolt some sense back into her head. Because Will, dressed in a formal white shirt and silk tie, was unbelievably beautiful. How on earth was she going to be able to concentrate for the next week, with him working in the same room as her? How on earth was she going to be able to pay attention to a set of figures, when what she really wanted to do was rip his clothes off and—?

Focus, she reminded herself. They had fifteen minutes before they had to leave the house. 'Can I make you some toast?'

He chuckled. 'Does that count as cooking?'

'Even I can shove two bits of bread in a toaster. Or there's cereal, yoghurt, fruit…'

She wished she hadn't said that last word. Because it made her think of the way he'd fed her that strawberry and licked the juice from the corner of her mouth.

'Just help yourself to whatever you want,' she finished, hoping he hadn't noticed the sudden huskiness in her voice.

Will opted for toast. She didn't dare, knowing that the act of licking buttery fingers would only give her libido ideas. Fruit was worse still. Cereal, at least, was safe.

'So tell me about your job,' Will said, picking up the camera and zooming in on her.

'My job's auditing,' she said. 'Which is basically checking the client's systems to make sure everything's recorded properly, and that any stock or machinery or buildings are where they're supposed to be. So then we can be sure that the financial statements we make—the year-end accounts for a company—are accurate and complete.'

He smiled. 'That's the textbook definition. What does it mean in practice?'

'Anything from doing a stocktake in a walk-in freezer for a food company—where you learn that at minus forty degrees ink freezes so you have to use a pencil when ticking things off a schedule—through to checking that computer systems are handling stock in the right way. We're doing a manufacturing company this week, so we need to understand their production processes from start to finish—from the raw material coming in to the finished product you see on the shelves.' She shrugged. 'I suppose in your terms that'd be like seeing an overview of a garden, from the initial meeting with your client through to the last plant going in.'

'So you have people doing this for you, or you do it all yourself?'

'I prepare the testing plan and initial documents for the audit, and write up the final report,' she said. 'And I carry out the more complicated tests myself. But, yes, I have a team. And part of my job is to develop them and make sure any assignments I give them fit in with their training plan.'

'Who develops your career?'

'My boss,' she said. Not that it was being developed at the moment. The way things were going, she would be at a complete standstill until she could prove herself. 'Though I know where I want to be. Audit manager, head of department, then partner.' If she worked hard enough. Proved how flexible she was. Made her boss realise that she was an asset, not a liability. 'I'm doing an MBA from September.'

'You're taking a career break?'

She shook her head. 'I'm studying part time, a couple of evenings a week.'

'That's a tough schedule, doing an intensive course like that and a demanding full-time job at the same time,' he said softly. 'What about time for you?'

'The MBA *is* for me.' He didn't look convinced, and she sighed. 'Look, Will, it's what I want to do with my life. The only way to get there is to work hard.'

'And what about when you get where you want to be? What then?'

'Then I'll find a new challenge.'

He switched off the camera. 'What about getting married? Having kids? Or isn't that on the agenda?'

'It's not mandatory, Will.' She looked at him. 'What about you? Is it on your agenda?'

'Not at the moment. But if I meet someone and realise they're the one I want to grow old with…'

Amanda was shocked at the flash of jealousy. When this whole lifeswap thing was over, she and Will probably wouldn't see each other again. She didn't have any *right* to be jealous. But the idea of Will falling in love with someone…

…was probably the best thing for both of them, she told herself sternly. 'We'd better get going,' she said. 'I'll have a pile of mail in the office, not to mention a site visit to arrange.'

'You don't have a secretary?'

'Not until you make partner.' With a brass plate on her door and a plaque with her name on it in the car park.

* * *

As Will half-expected, Amanda insisted on doing the washing up and making the kitchen spotless before they left. He would've been quite happy just to stack the breakfast things next to the sink and deal with them after dinner. But this was her week, her rules.

The Tube was even worse than he'd expected. She'd said they would go in early to beat the rush hour. But already it was crowded—too cramped to talk. Not that you could hear a lot, exactly, over the noise of the train and the tinny sounds from people's headphones.

It was hot, sticky and smelly—and this was first thing in the morning. Will grimaced at the thought of what it was going to be like when they caught the Tube this evening, after people had spent a hot day at work and their deodorants had stopped functioning.

'You do this every single day?' he asked when they'd finally left the tube station behind and were walking to the Amanda's office in the City.

'Unless I'm out at a client's where it'd be easier to go by car, yes.'

He grimaced. 'Don't you hate it—that feeling of being hemmed in, squashed together with all those people in the tiniest little space?'

'It's why I go in early. To avoid the rush.'

'You mean, that wasn't the rush?'

'No.' She frowned. 'Will, it's not that bad. You get used to it.'

Absolutely not. He'd never get used to this.

At the office reception, they paused to get Will a temporary pass for the week. Then he discovered that her office was on the eighth floor—and she always took the stairs.

'It's a good way of keeping fit,' she said, 'in between gym sessions.'

'Hmm.' Walking up and down a flight of stairs in a tower block or going to the gym. He'd much rather be walking along the river-bank or in the green spaces of Cambridge with his dog, or doing some serious digging.

Amanda's office turned out to be open plan. There were low dividers between the desks; Will presumed they were meant to act as soundproofing, as well as somewhere for people to pin notes and memos.

And he could've guessed which desk was hers. Even though she'd been away from it for a week and her in-tray was piled high, her desk was neat. There were a couple of notices pinned to the divider, but no photographs of family or cut-out cartoon strips or pictures of hunky actors. No flowers or plant on her desk. Nothing to give a clue about Amanda as a person, the sort of things she liked.

Which was part of the problem, he thought. In business, she cut to the chase. With anything personal, she was reserved, giving nothing away. It would make it very hard for someone to strike up a conversation with her. Where would they start? Talking about the weather?

'My desk,' she said, somewhat unnecessarily. 'It's up to you if you want to work here with me or use someone else's desk while they're out at a client's for the day.'

'I'm meant to do what you do. So your desk it is,' he said.

There was just the tiniest glitter in her eyes. Interesting. So she was nervous of him again—and even more so here, in her world. Was she worried that he'd make ripples?

'I need to introduce you to everyone. We'll start with my team—we have a team meeting scheduled for nine.'

He nodded. 'Does everyone know about the lifeswap thing?'

'Only my boss. Everyone else thinks you're shadowing me for a week. Management for a large potential client.'

He raised an eyebrow. 'So you're telling fibs.'

'No. You *are* management,' she pointed out. 'And the nursery could be a potential client.'

'Daynes is a small, personal, family business. Not the sort of place that employs London professionals with London prices.'

'Okay, so it's not the whole truth. But I don't want people—' She broke off abruptly.

'What? You're ashamed of me?'

She sighed. 'No. If you must know, I don't like being teased.'

She really thought her colleagues would tease her about this? Then again, this was the world of high finance. Any possible weakness in a team member would be mercilessly picked on. It'd be disguised as teasing, having a laugh—but there'd be an edge to it. He remembered Helen having a row with his parents about it once, asking them why they hadn't stepped in and warned some of their staff they were going too far and telling them to back off, before the secretary concerned had gone off on long-term sick leave with depression.

Nothing had changed in this world in the last fifteen years, then.

'Nobody's going to tease you about me,' he promised. And if they tried, they'd answer to him.

'I need to check my emails. The coffee machine's at the end of the room, if you want one.' She took a card from her wallet and handed it to him. 'Get whatever you want. It works in the snack machine, as well.'

Will got her a coffee as well; she murmured her thanks, but she was already clearly focused on her work. He watched her, fascinated as she worked through first the emails and then the paperwork in her top tray. He'd never seen anyone deal with a pile of papers so quickly: she opened the envelope, scanned the contents swiftly and either binned it, put it in one of three folders on her desk, or made a note on her electronic to-do list.

'So you only touch each piece of paper once,' he commented.

She frowned. 'That's common sense. If it's important, think about what needs to be done and by when and put it on your to-do list so you can prioritise your day's work; if it's not, delegate it or bin it.'

At three minutes to nine, Amanda shepherded him into the meeting room, set up at the head of the table with her laptop in front of her and an agenda placed neatly in front of Will and the other three places. The files she'd had on her desk were neatly stacked beside her.

At one minute to nine, three people filed in. So was everyone in this firm a stickler for time like Amanda? Was it because they were so focused on facts and figures, everything had to be precise? And would she drive her team as hard as she drove herself?

'Morning, team. This is Will Daynes. He's shadowing me for a week,' she said. 'Will, this is Rhiannon, who's just done her final exams; Mark, who's halfway through; and Drew, who's been with us for a year.'

They all smiled politely at him and made some sort of greeting, which he returned with a heavy heart. He had a nasty feeling this week was going to be dull, dull, dull.

'Rhiannon, can you give me an update on last week?' Amanda asked. She made the odd note as her junior spoke, checked with all three if there had been any problems or if anything had come up where any of them felt they had a training need, then talked them through the week ahead.

Amanda didn't work on one job at a time, it seemed. There was one—like the manufacturing company—in planning, one in progress and one that needed to be written up. And he noted that she was careful to ask all three of her staff how their recent exams had gone—Rhiannon's final papers, Mark's Part Ones and Drew's graduate conversion course.

There was nothing he could teach her about organisation, planning and looking after staff, Will thought. She knew exactly what she was doing.

At least the meeting was short. Well, it would be—Amanda was in charge of the agenda and didn't like wasting time. By the end of it, everyone knew what they were doing and when.

Next up was a brief meeting with Amanda's boss. A man with very shiny shoes, a weak handshake, and long, thin arms and legs. A spider, Will thought, at the middle of the web, plotting and snaring. But Will managed to be polite and to crack the obvious jokes.

Then there was a quick tour of the department. Will noticed that Amanda was polite but brisk, wasting no time with personal chat. Nobody asked her how her week off had been, he noted. She'd told him she didn't fit in; now he could see why. Or had she simply stopped making the effort to be sociable after a few rebuffs?

And then work. Going through files and cross-checking references. Will was bored to tears within half an hour.

'Who's responsible for the plants around here?' he asked.

'Internal landscape firm,' she said, still working through her files.

'They haven't been properly cared for. Some of them are in the wrong aspect and it looks to me as if the watering's been sloppy. When were they last fed?'

Amanda looked up from her desk. 'You hate this, don't you?'

He almost said yes—until he saw the look in her eyes. If he told her what he really thought, he had a feeling she'd take it personally. And it wasn't Amanda that was the problem—it was her lifestyle. 'I just noticed the plants.' He lowered his voice. 'Professional interest. Why aren't there any plants on your desk?'

'Because I'm rubbish with them,' she replied, her voice equally low.

'You need them to soak up radiation and what-have-you from your computer.'

She narrowed her eyes and gave the tiniest, impatient shake of her head. 'I'm fine. Stop fussing.'

Will managed to get through the next hour, thanks to two strong coffees. And then he needed some fresh air.

'Cabin'd, cribb'd, confin'd.' He grimaced into the video camera. 'Not bound to saucy doubts and fears, I admit. But I can't bear being stuck in an office like this. Nobody talks to each other here—they all talk *at* each other. Okay, so maybe in the garden centre they waste a few minutes yakking about whatever they saw on TV or read in the papers yesterday, but at least they talk to each other. At least there's teamwork. Here, it's all competition.'

Lunchtime was even worse. 'Aren't you having a break?' he asked.

Amanda stared at him as if he'd grown two heads. 'I've been away for a week, I've got an audit to plan and we're out at a client's tomorrow. I don't have *time* for a break, Will.'

'The way you work, you probably could do all that with your eyes closed.'

Bad choice of phrase. It reminded him too much of the evening when she'd closed her eyes and let him feed her, let him tempt her with tastes. When he'd kissed her properly, and she'd kissed him back. He dragged his thoughts back to the present with difficulty. 'What do you do for lunch?'

'Vending machine. In the corridor.'

'You're kidding.' Please, let her tell him she was kidding. 'You mean white bread that tastes like cardboard and a plasticky filling that's been stuck in a machine all day?'

She rolled her eyes. 'It's chilled and the packages are sealed. It's not going to make you ill.'

He wasn't so sure.

The afternoon dragged even more. For the first time in his life, Will found himself clock-watching. He couldn't remember ever being this bored. It wasn't that he couldn't do the tasks Amanda set him—he could—but they just didn't hold his interest. It felt like being on a treadmill, going on and on and on with no end or purpose in sight.

He noticed people leaving the office. Some went on the dot of five; others, clearly wanting to be seen to be keen, stayed until six. Amanda waited until ten to seven before calling it a day.

'Ever thought that maybe if you work fewer hours, you'll be fresher and work at a faster pace so you'll get the same amount of work done in a shorter time?' he asked.

She smiled. 'You're the one who was complaining about the Tube this morning. If you really want to travel home in the middle of the rush hour…'

'Hmm.'

And then she made it worse by calling in at the supermarket on the way back to her flat. She put two TV dinners and a ready-prepared salad in the wire basket.

'You're not serious,' he said. She had to be teasing him. She wasn't really expecting him to eat that stuff…was she?

She raised an eyebrow. 'My week, my rules.'

Oh, Lord. He was *never* going to survive this week. 'Is it really that much effort to chop salad?' he asked.

'Yes. Stop being such a food snob.'

It tasted as bad as he'd expected, but he forced it down and nagged her into letting him do the washing up.

And, just when he thought she was going to relax, out came some textbooks.

'You're not surely going to work now?'

Another of those polite but distant smiles. 'I'm doing some preliminary stuff for my MBA.'

'Amanda, working at this pace really isn't good for you.'

'I'm fine. Stop nagging.' She frowned. 'Look, if you're bored, just flick through the channels on the telly or something.'

He picked up the camera and switched it on. 'I don't think you need to stop and smell the roses, Amanda,' he said quietly.

She didn't even look up from her book. 'Good.'

'I think,' he said softly, 'you need to stop and learn to *breathe*.'

CHAPTER TWELVE

To WILL'S relief, Tuesday was better. No horrible Tube journey, as they were driving out to visit a client and picking up Drew, the most junior member of the team, on the way. Amanda introduced them both to the finance manager, talked the client through what they were going to do, and then it was straight into the audit.

'So we're all working separately?' Will asked.

'As part of the team, but, yes, we've all got set tasks. I've written a brief for each one,' Amanda told him, 'so all you have to do is follow it through and write up what you do and the results of the investigations.' For a moment, there was a hint of mischief in her smile. 'Unless you don't think you're up to it? I could find you something easier.'

That little flicker of feeling heartened him; and it amused him that she'd chosen to throw his own words back at him. 'If you can dig up ground elder, I can do this,' he retorted, returning the smile.

'Good. Just come and see me if you've got any questions,' she said.

There was one in his head, but now wasn't the time or place to ask it. *When are you going to kiss me again?*

Being busy was good. The more so because she'd assigned him tasks where he had to talk to people and get them to show him different processes. And, better still, she let him persuade her to go out for lunch at the kind of pub he liked best—the sort that served really, really good food.

Though she kept the conversation focused very firmly on work, he noticed. 'How did it go, this morning?' she asked.

'No problem,' Will said with a smile.

'Okay.' Drew didn't sound convinced, and Amanda zeroed in on that.

'What's up?' she asked.

Drew grimaced. 'Those invoices you told me to look at—well, the woman who deals with them is a real dragon. She's bitten my head off every time I've asked—she won't do a thing to help.'

After a day and a half of Drew, Will had a pretty good idea why. 'Ever thought,' he asked, 'of putting yourself in her shoes?'

Drew frowned. 'How do you mean?'

'You're an auditor. That means you're checking what she does. Like anyone who has the auditors in, she's scared that maybe you'll find something wrong and she'll lose her job.'

Drew scoffed. 'That's ridiculous—though if she does do things wrong then maybe she shouldn't be doing the job.'

'That,' Will said in near disbelief, 'is the most callous thing I've ever heard. Does Amanda treat *you* like that?'

There was a slight stain of colour on the younger man's cheeks. 'Well, no.' He gave her a sidelong look. 'But she does check up on things more than any of the other seniors do.'

'Because the buck stops with me,' Amanda said. 'And rule number one is that you're *always* polite to clients. When it comes to losing jobs, consider this: if you upset the staff on an audit, they might complain about you. Complaints could mean our firm loses the job to someone else next year. If we lose a certain number of clients, we'll have to downsize. Try extrapolating that.'

Drew thought about it. 'You lose your job?' he asked.

Amanda smiled thinly. 'As would my team.'

Drew shook his head. 'They couldn't get rid of *me*. I'm on a training contract,' he said loftily.

'It doesn't make you safe. Think about it. And I'm going to add a course on interpersonal skills to your training plan.'

Drew gave her a speaking look. Will, just about keeping a lid on his impatience, said, 'You might find it helpful to lose the attitude. Amanda's interpersonal skills are fine.'

Drew scoffed. 'Yeah, well, you would say that.'

Amanda's cheeks flamed as she caught the implication.

Will said very softly, 'What goes around, comes around. If you treat other people with that kind of contempt, they'll have no respect for you. Would you want *your* juniors gossiping about you behind your back when you're audit senior?'

Drew shifted in his seat. 'Well, no.'

'Think about it,' Will advised sagely. 'And I'm going with you to see this woman, this afternoon. Watch and learn.'

Hang on, Amanda thought, *I'm* supposed to be teaching *Will* this week—and Drew's *my* responsibility. Will seemed to have taken over the teaching role. Though she had to admit he was better with people than she was. And the way he'd stood up for her against Drew's little snipes sent a warm glow through her whole body.

After lunch, Will did exactly what he'd said, and returned to Amanda alone.

'What happened?' she asked.

He shrugged. 'Drew is looking through the papers he wanted to see.'

The papers the woman apparently hadn't wanted to give him earlier. 'So what happened?'

'I asked for him,' Will explained. 'The poor woman was clearly run off her feet and didn't need the added irritation of having to sift through a pile of papers for someone who was swaggering around with a superiority complex. So I did a deal with her—I made her a cup of coffee and she showed me where the invoices were. I promised we wouldn't muddle up the order of the papers and we'd put everything back where we found them. And then I got Drew to talk me through exactly what I just did and why that approach worked better. He doesn't like me very much right now—and that's completely mutual, by the way—but I think his behaviour's going to improve.'

'Thanks, Will.' She smiled wryly at him. 'I find managing a team a bit tough sometimes.'

'With attitudes like that, I'm not surprised. Drew clearly believes that he's better than everyone else because he's been to university or got a job while his mates are still looking at their student loans and worrying. Whereas in the real world, that's not the case.' Will shrugged. 'He just needs the edges smoothed off him, and that'll happen, given time.'

'He was right about one thing, though,' she admitted. 'My own interpersonal skills aren't exactly brilliant.'

'You're more comfortable with figures than people, yes. But that's no excuse for the way he behaved to you.' Will raised an eyebrow. 'I still can't believe what you said to him in the pub. "Try extrapolating that." It's not the kind of word I'd expect to hear in everyday conversation.' He gestured to the audit schedules next to her. 'But then again, I can see the other words you're using here. Scrutinise…that's quite a threatening word,' he said thoughtfully.

'So are the alternatives: inspect, examine, analyse, check. And this is a formal business document—one that might have to stand up in a court of law—so don't suggest something like "give the purchase ledger the once-over."'

'As if I would.' His eyes twinkled. 'Okay, boss. Next task.'

The afternoon went by quickly, but, because they'd eaten out, Amanda decreed a sandwich would do for their evening meal. It wasn't the kind of bread or ham Will was used to, but he supposed he should consider himself lucky it wasn't one of the vacuum-packed sandwiches they'd had for lunch the day before.

She must have caught the distaste in his expression, because she sighed. 'Will, you're being such a snob. Most people eat sand-wiches just like this.'

'I'm not being a snob. I'm just used to…' he knew he had to be careful about the way he phrased it, because he didn't want to hurt her '…less processed food,' he finished.

'My week, my rules,' she reminded him.

Amanda worked on her studies again that evening, while Will sprawled on the sofa with a book and his MP3 player. And at the end of the evening he delivered his verdict to the camera. 'She's driven. Absolutely driven. Though I can't work out *why*.'

Unless she was trying to avoid being too close to him, in case last Thursday evening repeated itself? Not that he'd say that on screen.

'She doesn't let people get close. Although I'm shadowing her, the barriers between us are growing thicker by the minute. And I have no idea where to start breaking them down.' He switched off the camera.

Actually, he did have one idea. But that was most definitely not for sharing with anyone except Amanda. And if he got it wrong, the barriers between them would not only be enormous, they'd also be covered in anti-climb paint.

The next morning, Will and Amanda left the flat an hour earlier. The Tube was marginally better—either that, Will thought, or he was already getting used to the squash.

'So this gym's near your office?' he asked.

She nodded. 'It means I can go on the way home—which I normally do on Fridays—or do an early session and have enough time to cool down before work.'

The idea of being squashed into a hot, sticky train after a workout really didn't bear thinking about. Will was grateful that the gym was within walking distance of Amanda's office.

Amanda arranged a temporary pass for him as her guest.

'Do you go to a gym regularly, or should I book you an induction course in the weights room?' the receptionist asked.

No to both, Will thought. 'Are there any classes?' he asked. 'Circuit training or what-have-you?'

The receptionist checked the gym schedule. 'There's a spinning class in ten minutes.'

'Spinning?'

'A forty-five-minute static cycling workout to music,' she explained.

Bicycles were the main form of transport in Cambridge, though Will was more used to walking or punting. It had been a while since he'd done any cycling. 'I'll give it a go,' he said with a smile. 'Amanda, are you going to join me?'

'No. I have a routine.'

He grinned as they walked to the changing rooms. 'I was right, then—you're way too much of a control freak to take a class.'

She glowered at him and pushed open the door to the ladies' changing rooms.

Will got changed faster than she did and was waiting outside, leaning against the wall, when she emerged.

In knee-length clingy shorts and a close-fitting T-shirt that showed all her curves, she looked mouthwatering.

And he knew exactly how she tasted.

He shoved the thought to the back of his mind. If he started thinking about that kiss, he'd end up doing something stupid. Like pinning her to the wall and kissing her until they both forgot where they were—and the gossip machine would go into overdrive. Someone as private as Amanda would just hate being the subject of office gossip, especially because a slip-up from her would be so rare that it would be the top talking point in the office for days instead of blowing over quickly. And hadn't she already told him she hated being teased?

'That was an inflammatory comment earlier and I take it back,' he said.

'Apologies normally contain the S word,' she said, her voice crisp.

'Sorry,' he said, meaning it. 'But this class sounds like fun. Why not come and do it with me?'

He honestly hadn't meant to make an innuendo. But Amanda clearly took it that way, because she blushed. Really blushed. 'I have a personalised workout that suits me. As they say, if it ain't broke, why fix it?'

For a moment, he was tempted to goad her into it—make clucking noises or something. But Amanda wasn't the easily manipulated sort. And that blush had made him feel a hell of a lot better because now he knew for sure that he wasn't alone in these feelings. That maybe there was a chance. 'See you after class, then,' he said.

'Hey. You're forgetting something.'

'What?'

She handed him a bottle of water. 'Hydration.'

She'd brought a drink especially for him? The thought warmed him. 'Thanks.' He wanted to hug her, but her expression said 'keep off'. Clearly here, just as much as at work, she was this self-contained little island.

He picked a bike smack in the centre of the room, where he'd still be able to see the instructor but could also see people around him and maybe follow them if he got lost in the middle of a routine.

'Wow—we actually have a man in the class today,' a woman said, walking over to him and smiling. 'I'm the instructor.'

He smiled back. 'Will Daynes.'

'Is this your first spinning class?' At his 'yes', she talked him through how the resistance switch on the bike worked. 'Don't feel you have to compete with other people,' she warned. 'The only person who will see what your resistance level is will be you. So just do what's right for you—if it's too much, then turn the resistance down and don't try to be a hero about it.'

Will laughed. 'I know the sort of guy you mean. That's not how I work.'

'Good.' She gave him an approving look. 'We warm up first with some low resistance, and then do a "hill climb"—you turn up the resistance as you go, to make it feel as if you're climbing a hill. Some songs, you'll stand up and pedal for some counts and sit down for others.'

'Stand up on a bike? Won't it fall over?' Will asked.

'No, because a spinning bike has a heavier frame and fly-wheel,' she reassured him. 'At the end, we slow everything back down to normal and finish the cool-down routine with arm stretches and leg stretches. There aren't any brakes on the bike, so you'll have to slow your pedalling down to stop.'

'So how's a spinning class better for you than going for a ride on an ordinary bike?' he asked.

'In London? No traffic, for starters.' She laughed. 'And you can burn anything from five hundred to seven hundred calories in a class. Have you got a drink?'

'Yep.'

'Good. Enjoy the class.' She nodded at the towel beside his bike. 'And you'll need that afterwards.'

It was a much more intensive workout than he'd expected, but the adrenalin kicked in. Even though the music wasn't quite to his taste, the pounding dance track was perfect for keeping them all in rhythm. And after the cool-down, he noticed everyone used the towel placed next to the bike to wipe it down; he followed suit.

'Did you enjoy it?' the woman on the bike next to his asked.

'More than I expected,' he admitted. 'I definitely feel that I've done a workout. How about you?'

'It's brilliant. I've been coming for three months now,' another woman added, walking over to join them. 'So are you coming back?'

'I'm not sure,' Will said. 'I'm only in London for a week.'

'Pity,' the first woman said with a smile. 'Here on business?'

'Yes.'

'Nothing worse than being stuck in a hotel on your own at the end of the day,' the second woman said as they walked back towards the changing rooms. 'Look, there's a group of us going to the pub tonight. Why don't you come along?'

Give me strength, Amanda thought, coming from the weights room and overhearing the last bit. Will had been in the gym barely an hour and already there were women flocking round him. Asking him out, too.

She'd been pretty much ignoring him in the evenings, concentrating on her studies, so she wouldn't blame him for accepting the invitation. But there was a tight knot of disappointment in her stomach at the thought of being on her own.

Crazy. She liked her life the way it was. Will Daynes was way too spontaneous for her comfort. And it wasn't as if he was anything more than a business associate anyway. She shouldn't start feeling possessive about him. Or jealous.

'That's really sweet of you to ask,' Will said, 'but I'm not actually on my own. I'm with a colleague.'

The tall, statuesque brunette actually fluttered her eyelashes at him, Amanda noted with disgust. 'Bring him with you.'

'Her, actually,' Will corrected with a smile.

Uh-oh. She hadn't expected him to bring her into it. Was he going to say yes for both of them? The idea of spending an entire evening in a noisy pub with a crowd of people she didn't even know—an evening when she could be preparing for her MBA course—was just hideous. He wouldn't do that to her…would he?

'I'm sorry, we've already promised to be somewhere tonight. But the offer's really appreciated—isn't it, Mands?' he asked, looking over at her and smiling.

Mands? That was a new one on her. And it was even worse than Dee's version of her name. She forced a smile to her face. 'Hi, Will. And, yes, you're right.' About one thing. 'The offer's appreciated.' The rest of it was a complete fabrication. Why had he lied? And if he could lie that convincingly…

No. She didn't want to start extrapolating that.

'Good workout, Mands?' he asked.

To her utter shock, Will slid his arm round her shoulders. And her brain turned to mush. What was the question? 'Mmm,' she said, hoping the response would cover the fact that she'd completely lost the plot.

'So are you up in London for the week, too?' one of the women asked.

She shook her head. 'I work round the corner.'

'I haven't seen you at any of the classes before,' the woman remarked.

'I, um, tend to use the weight room.'

'Uh-huh.'

Being the centre of attention was just…horrible, Amanda thought. The other women were clearly looking at her and wondering what on earth someone as charming and sophisticated as Will was doing with someone like her. Colleagues, they might have swallowed. But the way he'd draped that casual arm round her more or less said they were an item.

And nobody believed him.

Why did that hurt so much?

'We're going to be late for work,' she muttered to Will. 'I need a shower.'

His thumb caressed the back of her neck as he moved his arm away, sending a shiver down her spine. 'See you in a minute,' he said, giving her a slow, sexy smile that told everyone around them that he'd much rather be having the shower with her.

Lord, the *embarrassment* of people knowing that. And even when she turned the temperature of the water right down, it couldn't cool the heat in her face.

She was still hot and bothered when she'd dressed and walked out of the changing rooms to find Will already waiting for her.

'Okay?' he asked.

'Mmm,' she said, meaning *not on your life*.

When they'd left the gym, she said softly, 'You can't help yourself, can you?'

'What?'

'Flirting. In the gym.'

He blinked. 'I wasn't flirting. Those women were just being friendly.'

'To you, yes.' She hadn't actually meant flirting with *them*. She'd meant the way he'd flirted with her. The hand-and-eye stuff. The way he'd stroked the back of her neck.

He raised an eyebrow. 'Hmm. That sounds like jealousy.'

'Of course it isn't,' she said crossly.

Will rubbed his nose, and she knew exactly what he was thinking. Pinocchio. It goaded her into saying, 'You're meant to be shadowing me, not flirting.' The moment the words left her mouth, she regretted them. The last time she'd accused him of flirting, he'd kissed her. A covert glance at his face told her he remembered, too.

Oh, Lord, she had to get thoughts of kissing out of her head, or else she was going to go crazy.

'And don't call me "Mands",' she said.

'Why not?' Mischief was written all over his face. 'It's cute.'

'It's irritating,' she corrected. 'My name is Amanda.'

'*Amanda.*'

How did he manage to make the word sound like a caress sliding over her skin? She needed more than just coffee to kick-start her brain cells this morning before work. She needed something to keep her libido where it belonged.

Under control.

Another interminable day in the office. Will lasted half a morning before he snapped and started sorting out the plants.

Amanda didn't say anything, but there was a note on his place on her desk in her neat, precise handwriting when he returned. *What are you doing?*

Sorting out the plants. I told you on Monday, they're not being watered properly and they were in the wrong aspect. They'll grow now, he scribbled and shoved the note back to her.

You're supposed to be shadowing me.

He knew that. *Could you have stood by if I'd been doing something seriously wrong in accountancy terms?*

Probably not.

Exactly. QED.

She didn't reply. Just continued working.

He rather liked this little game. Private messages. What would she do if he wrote 'I want to kiss you'?

Probably run a mile.

But there was another way…He scribbled her another note. *Let's have lunch out today.* Before he got too stir crazy. *Find a park somewhere near.*

There isn't one, came the reply. *Anyway, it's too hot. The office is air conditioned.*

He should've expected that. Amanda wasn't the sort to play hooky and go to the park for a picnic lunch. She'd been horrified when he'd taken her to the Botanical Gardens for the afternoon.

Though she'd also kissed him…

He really ought to stop thinking about that, or he'd make a stupid mistake—and he didn't want her having to cover for him. But she was sitting so close to him, he could smell her perfume. So close that his knee could press against hers.

He'd deliberately agreed to sit at her desk with the aim of unsettling her, and making her aware of his presence. It looked as if he was hoist with his own petard.

Somehow he got through the rest of the morning, a vacuum-packed sandwich at their desk for lunch, and an interminable afternoon. But when Amanda dragged him over to the chiller cabinet in the supermarket, pointed to the TV dinners and asked him which one he'd like that evening, he lost it.

'That's it. We're breaking the rules.'

She frowned. 'How do you mean?'

'I know I'm meant to be shadowing you, but I can't eat this stuff. I'm cooking for you tonight.'

'But—'

'No arguments, Amanda. We're doing this one my way.' He took the wire basket from her, shepherded her round the shop, filled the basket with salmon and fresh vegetables, and paid before she had the chance to protest.

'I'll pay you back,' she said as he nudged her out of the door.

'Believe me, not having to eat the stuff you serve up is payment enough,' he said feelingly.

She must have realised he'd reached his limit, because she didn't argue once, all the way back to her flat.

'Now. Cookery lesson,' he said when they were in her kitchen. 'Turn on oven. Take one glass dish.' He suited his actions to the words. 'Tear off one big piece of foil. Put salmon in the middle. Put a tiny bit of butter on the top and a grind of black pepper. Fold foil like so. Put in oven.' He closed the oven door and leaned against the worktop with his arms folded. 'That's hardly any more work than preparing one of those vile ready meals—and you don't have unbiodegradable rubbish to dispose of, either.'

She frowned. 'Are you trying to make me feel guilty about carbon footprints and what-have-you?'

'No. I'm trying to get you to eat properly. You put this in the oven and leave it for thirty minutes—and you can do the same with a boneless chicken breast or a pork loin steak. Use lemon juice and herbs, or a bit of bottled marinade, if you want to ring the changes. Get an electric steamer and put your veg on at the same time, and they'll all be ready together.' He sighed, exasperated that she didn't see it. 'It's no more difficult than putting a plastic tray into the oven.'

Her jaw set. 'I don't have time.'

'Five minutes. That's all it takes.'

'I don't see the point of cooking.'

'Or eating? I thought I'd already taught you that food's more than fuel.'

Her pupils expanded; clearly she was remembering that lesson in taste in his back garden. 'That's in your world, Will.' She dragged in a breath. 'This is mine.'

A world where he didn't fit.

Somehow they'd have to find a place to compromise. Though right now he wasn't sure where.

CHAPTER THIRTEEN

'AH, AMANDA—just the woman I wanted.' Ed perched on the edge of her desk and smiled at her.

In other words, he was running late on an audit and wanted to borrow a couple of her juniors. She flapped her hand casually at him. 'Fine. I'll give you a note of their charge codes for your budget sheet.'

He laughed. 'I don't always want to borrow your juniors, you know.'

Oh, yes, he did. It was just about the only time he ever bothered with her.

'What can I do for you, then?' she asked, pinning her politest smile to her face.

'I wondered if you wanted to come out for a meal with us after work tonight. There's a few of us going for Chinese.'

She stared at him, not quite believing what she'd just heard. Since when did Ed ever include her in invitations to meals out? 'Chinese?'

'They do other stuff if you don't like Chinese,' he said quickly. 'Will said to check with you.'

So that was it. She ignored the tight little knot of hurt in her stomach. They wanted Will to go, and he'd probably said something about not going without her. It was exactly the same way that those women in the gym had invited him out for a drink and he'd made sure that the invite had included her. 'I—um—'

'You've had him to yourself every evening this week,' Ed pointed out, grinning.

'He's shadowing me.'

'At work, yes.' Ed's grin broadened. 'Outside...well...' He winked.

He thought she and Will were…? She lifted her chin. 'I don't know what you're implying, but we're just colleagues.'

'Oh, come *on*, Amanda. The rest of the women in the office have got the hots for him and you're spending all day, every day, with him. Don't tell me he hasn't managed to melt the ice in your veins yet.'

She knew he was trying to goad her into a reaction, and that made her just about capable of resisting the urge to slap him. 'My private life,' she said coolly, 'isn't up for discussion. I've already told you he's a colleague. If you want to make ridiculous speculations, I suggest you do it on your own time rather than the firm's. Now, if you don't mind, some of us have work to do.'

Ed shrugged and hauled himself off her desk. 'Suit yourself.'

'I will.' She made a show of concentrating on her work, but inside she was fuming. How come Ed always got away with it? He'd failed his exams twice, but he'd still been promoted to audit manager, whereas she'd passed hers with top marks and was still stuck exactly where she was.

And now he was spreading rumours about her.

'I'm glad that's a pencil and not a dagger.'

She looked up at the sound of his voice. 'Oh. Will.'

'You okay?' he asked.

'Fine.' If you didn't include wanting to murder someone. 'If you want to go for that Chinese meal tonight, that's fine. I'll give you my spare key.'

'Don't you want to go?'

'I have a meeting. Dinner with a client.'

He raised an eyebrow. 'That wasn't on the schedule.'

'Late amendment.'

'Sounds like an excuse.'

She sighed. 'You know as well as I do, I don't fit in.'

'And if you don't make the effort, how are you ever going to fit in?' he asked softly.

'Maybe,' she said, her fingers tightening round the pencil again, 'I don't want to. Maybe I'm perfectly fine as I am.'

'Hmm. Come with me.'

'Where?'

'Meeting room.' He unfolded her fingers from the pencil, took her hand and tugged her to her feet. Then he took a file from her desk.

'What's that for?'

'Discussion,' he said, ushering her over to the meeting room and closing the door behind them. He put the file on the desk, unopened. 'Right. Now you're going to tell me what's really wrong.'

'Nothing.'

'Okay. Let me put this another way. If I have a tree with scale and I don't do anything about it, it'll spread and feed on the sap until the leaves go yellow and the tree starts to die. If I treat the problem, I'll have a healthy tree.'

She frowned. 'And?'

'It's the same for you. Whatever's upsetting you, if you keep it to yourself, it's going to grow and grow and make you feel worse. Tell me what's wrong, and that's half the problem solved.'

She felt a muscle flicker in her jaw. 'I told you before, I hate people gossiping about me.'

'Who's gossiping?'

'Ed. He thinks you and I are…' Her voice faded. Said aloud, it would sound even more ridiculous.

'Maybe,' Will said, 'we should give him something to talk about.'

Before she had any idea what Will was going to do, he picked her up, set her on the edge of the table, slid one hand to the base of her spine to press her against him and the other at the nape of her neck, and kissed her.

Stars exploded in her head, and she slid her hands into his hair and kissed him back. The whole of London vanished—the whole of the world, even, because Amanda wasn't aware of anything else right at that moment except Will and the way his mouth was teasing a response from her.

When he broke the kiss, she was practically hyperventilating.

And then she remembered where they were. In the meeting room. Where anyone could've looked through the narrow glass pane in the door and seen them kissing.

Especially Ed.

The office grapevine would go crazy.

'We're in the *office*,' she hissed. 'I don't *do* this sort of thing at work.' She didn't exactly do it outside, either, but that was another matter.

Will ran the pad of his thumb along her lower lip, making her shiver with need. 'Neither do I. But I've been fantasising about this for a week.' His eyes glowed gold with desire. 'Sweeping everything off the desk and putting you in its place and kissing you.'

In her office, there was a clear desk policy, so he didn't need to sweep any papers aside. In his… 'It'd take you a week to *clear* your desk.'

He laughed. 'Ever heard of the volcano principle? If a piece of paper is important enough it'll make its way to the top of the pile.'

'More like it'll take you hours to find anything. All you need to do is file a little tiny bit a day; then it won't build up and be an impossible task.'

'Stop trying to organise me.' He stopped her wriggling off the table by the simple means of resting his palms on her thighs. The thoughts that roused in her brain were enough to keep her absolutely still.

'There's nothing wrong with my filing system,' he said.

'Your filing system is the passenger footwell in your car,' she pointed out.

'And that's a problem how, exactly?'

Could he really not see it?

'Aren't you going to tell me?' he asked, stealing another kiss.

That kiss had leached away all coherent thought. She couldn't for the life of her remember the logical argument she had planned. She shook her head and smiled wryly. 'Will, you're impossible.'

'But you're smiling now.' He stroked her cheek. 'So I've achieved my objectives for the day.'

She frowned. 'What objectives?' Was kissing her some kind of objective? And then a seriously nasty thought wormed into her mind. Ed and his cronies were competing with each other to see who could play the field hardest—and they'd asked Will to go on this meal out. And Ed had made that crack about Will melting the ice in her veins. She didn't think Will was like them…but then again, she didn't understand the male bonding process at all. Just please, please don't say he had a bet with one of them about getting her into bed. Because, if that happened, she'd never live it down—and she'd never forgive him for betraying her.

'I'm just following your business principles and setting objectives, that's all,' he said.

Heat prickled at the back of her neck. Heat and adrenalin and the tiniest bit of fear. 'What objectives?' she asked again.

'Firstly, to make you smile. And, secondly, to kiss you—for long enough to make you kiss me back.'

She felt her face flame. He was right. That was exactly what she'd done. Forgotten where she was and kissed him back. 'Why did you want to kiss me?'

He looked at her in obvious disbelief. 'Do you really not know?'

'I wouldn't be asking, otherwise.'

He rolled his eyes. 'I want to kiss you, Amanda, because I'm attracted to you. Extremely attracted. And if you don't believe me…' He slid his hands under her buttocks and pulled her against him so she was left in absolutely no doubt about his arousal.

She'd thought her face had felt hot earlier. Now, her temperature had gone beyond scorching.

Clearly it showed, because he smiled. 'Do you know how sexy you look when you blush?'

With difficulty, she dragged her thoughts together. 'Will, I can't do this. We're in the office. And I have a client meeting in ten minutes.'

'Shame.' He leaned forward and whispered in her ear, 'Ten minutes isn't anywhere near long enough to do what I want to do with you.'

Oh, Lord. The ideas that he put into her head. She felt as if she were spiking a fever.

'I need much, *much* longer,' he drawled.

Oh-h-h.

She clung to the last shreds of coherence. She had a client meeting. Will had just kissed her stupid. And it probably showed. She couldn't walk out of here and face Ed and the others. 'I…I need to fix my lipstick.'

'You look lovely as you are.' He tucked a strand of hair behind her ear. 'Relax.'

That was just the problem. She couldn't. Didn't know *how*.

'I have to prepare for this meeting, Will. It's important.'

'Okay. This thing between us isn't going away. It can wait until later.' He held her gaze. 'And that's a promise, Amanda.'

Amanda actually had to force herself to concentrate during the client meeting. She certainly didn't dare meet Will's eye. Because she knew what she'd see there: a heat that would make a matching need rise in her own body.

She absolutely refused to set foot outside the office over lunch. Knowing Will, he'd checked out the nearest park on the Internet and was planning to whisk her off for a picnic or something. She didn't have *time* for that.

Ha. More like she was too scared, she admitted silently. The last time they'd been in a garden together, she'd ended up naked to the waist. She didn't think he'd go that far in a public place—but then again, the way he'd made her feel in the meeting room earlier that morning, she couldn't trust herself.

He made no comment and disappeared. But when he came back, he brought her a little box of strawberries. Ready-to-eat, hulled and washed strawberries. The fruit he'd teased her with that evening in his garden.

And she thought of it every time she ate one of the tiny, sweet fruits.

She was pretty sure he was thinking of it, too—because that hungry look was back in his eyes.

Dinner was murder. She had no idea what anyone was talking about, because Will was sitting opposite her. Will, who had the sexiest smile in the world. Will, whose eyes promised her that he was going to continue where he'd left off last time over the strawberries.

He didn't touch her. He didn't have to. It was the way he held her gaze as he bit into the dark chocolate thin that accompanied their coffee.

Tasting it the way he planned to taste her.

He still didn't touch her all the way to the Tube. But then he sat next to her, so close that his thigh rested against hers.

'So, beautiful lady, what now?'

She frowned. 'What did you call me?'

He smiled. 'You heard. Beautiful.'

Her frown deepened. 'But I'm not—I'm just ordinary.'

'No, you're not. Has nobody ever told you how cute you are?'

Cute? It wasn't a word anyone ever used around her.

The tip of his finger traced the curve of her eyebrows. 'Your eyes are the same colour as the Fenland sky in early spring,' he whispered. 'And your mouth's a perfect cupid's bow. When you smile, it makes your whole face light up. And it makes me want to do this.' He leaned over and kissed her very lightly on the lips, then pulled back far enough so she could see his eyes. See the sincerity.

'We've both been fighting it. Decided we're too different for it to work between us. But I've been thinking. Maybe we've got it wrong,' he said. 'Maybe it's more that our differences make us balanced. That we complement each other.'

Was he suggesting…? But no. It couldn't work out between them. He loathed the city and no way could she bury herself in a backwater. Even for Will. She'd seen what it had done to her mother—it would do the same to her.

As if he saw her doubts surfacing, Will leaned forward again, and drew a trail of kisses to her ear. 'I want to do more than just kiss you. A lot more. Because I know what it's like to be half-naked with you. And I really, really want to be completely naked with you.' He nuzzled the sensitive spot behind her ear. 'Just you and me and nothing in between,' he whispered.

'You're drunk,' she said shakily.

'Not on one glass of wine. And you didn't drink much, either. This isn't alcohol.' He nibbled her earlobe. 'This is pheromones. Much, much headier stuff.'

'Sex—' she could barely drag the word out '—is overrated.'

'Is it, now?' His eyes glittered. 'Then I dare you.'

She folded her arms. 'I don't take dares.'

'Live dangerously for once,' he said, his voice husky. 'I dare you to find out—with me.'

Could she? Should she?

'If you're worried about protection,' he added softly, 'don't be. I'll take care of you.'

Of course he'd carry condoms. A man as gorgeous as Will Daynes had women throwing themselves at him all the time. She'd seen the way every single female in the office had looked at him. Not to mention the gym, the pub, even the supermarket. Will turned heads.

As if he'd guessed her thoughts, he said, 'Just for the record, I'm picky. I don't sleep with all my girlfriends.'

'I'm not your girlfriend.'

He didn't deny it, she noticed. Well, she'd known for a while she wasn't girlfriend material. And it didn't bother her because she didn't need distracting from her career goals. She already had her life planned out the way she wanted it.

'Last week you were my shadow,' he said. 'This week, I'm yours.'

Okay. That summed up the situation very nicely.

'But tonight, I want you to be my lover.'

Could she? *Should* she?

'Say yes,' he murmured next to her ear.

His breath was warm against her skin; a shiver of longing rippled down her spine. *Live dangerously for once.*

'Yes,' she whispered.

He didn't say anything, but the hot look in his eyes told her everything she needed to know. She couldn't even remember getting off the Tube and walking back to her flat with him.

The second the door had closed behind them, he was kissing her. Really kissing her. The kind of kiss she'd only ever seen in a girly movie when Dee dragged her off to the cinema. Hot and wet and open-mouthed. Ripping each other's clothes off and not caring where the garments landed. Pressing each other against walls and doors. Urgent and needy and hot.

Will picked her up, carried her to her room, and kicked the door open, still kissing her. Stripped her of the last bits of lacy underwear. Got rid of his own clothes. And then they were skin to skin, belly to belly, thigh to thigh.

She couldn't remember ever wanting anything as much as she wanted Will, right here and right now. His teeth against her throat. His hands stroking her breasts and her belly and easing her thighs apart. The scorching desire in his eyes as he looked at her.

But as he nudged his thigh between hers, she froze.

Will stopped immediately. 'What's the matter, honey?' he asked. *Tell me what's wrong, and that's half the problem solved.*

Maybe, maybe not. But this was something he really ought to know. 'I'm not very good at this,' she admitted, her voice cracking.

Will stroked her face and kissed her so gently, so tenderly that her heart swelled. 'It's not a competition. It's teamwork,' he said.

'Teamwork?' she croaked.

'Uh-huh. You and I, we're on the same side. I want to find out how you like to be touched, what gives you pleasure, what makes you feel good.' He kissed her again. 'And I'm going to show you what I like, too.'

'I think I'm scared.'

She hadn't realised she'd spoken aloud until he told her huskily, 'There's no need. Because we're going to be very, very good together.' He rubbed the tip of his nose against hers. 'Trust me on this. And I'm going to start by kissing you all over.'

By the time he'd finished, she was quivering. And more desperate than she'd ever have believed possible. 'I want you,' she said, her voice shaking.

'Good. Because I want you, too. So much that I think I'm going to die if I don't…' Slowly, slowly, he eased his body into hers.

Filling her, easing the ache—and when he started to move, she stared at him in wonder. She'd always thought sex was overrated, but this was nothing like anything she'd ever known. The way his thrusts stoked her desire, built it higher and higher; the way he brought her closer and closer to the edge, little by little and kiss by kiss and push by push. She could feel heat radiating from the soles of her feet all the way up to the top of her head—and then suddenly she was falling, falling right over the edge.

'Will!'

His mouth jammed over hers, and she felt the answering surge of his body within hers.

Some time later, he whispered, 'Did I hurt you, honey? I'm sorry.'

Then she realised her face was wet. 'No.' She scrubbed the tears away with the back of her wrist, not wanting him to think she was weak. 'No, you didn't hurt me.'

He caught her hand, kissed the back of it and then kissed her tears away. 'Tell me, Amanda.'

They'd shared too much for her to be anything but honest with him. 'I didn't know it could be like this.'

He nuzzled his cheek against hers. 'Neither did I.'

No way. She wasn't swallowing that one. A man as gorgeous

as Will Daynes—one who managed to get women flocking round him within a few minutes of walking into a room—it wasn't possible that he'd never experienced something like that before. 'You've had plenty of girlfriends,' she said, her eyes narrowing.

'If you're asking, yes, I've dated and, yes, I've slept with my partners. But it's always been mutual and it's always been fun.' Then his eyes widened and he looked utterly shocked. 'Oh, my God. Have I just been completely insensitive? Are you telling me that was your first time?'

Her jaw set. 'I'm twenty-seven. I'm not *that* sad.'

He laughed, rolled over on to his back and pulled her into his arms so that her head was resting on his shoulder and his arm was curved round her waist. 'Honey, there's nothing sad about being a virgin at twenty-seven. It shows you value yourself—that you're choosy.' He kissed her shoulder. 'I'm sorry. I would have taken it a little slower if I'd realised.'

'I'm *not* a virgin,' she said through clenched teeth. 'I've slept with someone before.'

'And since then you've thought sex was overrated?'

Trust him to remember what she'd said to him on the Tube. And work out why. Embarrassed, she muttered, 'Yes.'

'Sounds to me as if he didn't take enough time.'

'How do you mean?'

'He didn't try to find out what made you feel good. So he wasn't doing it right.'

'So it wasn't me?' The words slipped out before she could stop them.

He tightened his arms round her. 'No, it most definitely wasn't you. Was that what he said?'

Oh, Lord. She'd forgotten how good Will was at reading people. Of course he'd work it out. She turned her face away, not wanting him to see the humiliation and hurt the memories dragged back.

'Look at me, Amanda.'

His voice was so gentle, so soft, she did so.

'He lied. It wasn't you.' He stroked her face. 'So here you are, thinking that you don't fit anywhere and you're useless with people and no good at sex.'

'Don't pull your punches, do you?' He'd homed in on everything that was wrong in her life. Everything that was wrong with her.

'It's how you see yourself. Not the way I see you.' He kissed the tip of her nose. 'You fit me perfectly.'

'How? How, when we're so different?'

'Complementary.' Another kiss, at the corner of her mouth. 'It works. And you're not useless with people. You sparkled tonight, at dinner.'

Had she? She couldn't remember a thing about the evening. Except Will.

'When you let go, relax, people like being around you. Then they're not scared they'll fail to meet your standards,' he told her. 'You're clever and you're good company. Just relax, believe in yourself and they won't reject you.'

She felt the tears pooling in her eyes again. 'I hate this. I *never* cry.'

'Tears can be healing.' He kissed the other corner of her mouth. 'And then we have the third thing. This belief that you're no good at sex. Now, if that were true, neither of us would have climaxed. And I wouldn't have to go to the bathroom pretty shortly to deal with something.'

'Oh.' She hadn't thought of that.

'I'm not going to be long. And I'm not going to my own room tonight, either.' He brushed his mouth against hers. 'I'm coming back to you. Because I want to spend the entire night with you, Amanda. I want to hold you and fall asleep with you and wake with you in my arms.'

Even though she knew it was anatomically impossible, she could feel her heart melting.

'Hold that thought,' he whispered, brushing another kiss against her mouth. 'I won't be long.'

He was as good as his word. A couple of minutes later, he was spooned behind her, his arms wrapped round her and keeping her close to his body. She'd never felt more protected and warm and *loved* before.

Loved? No. He hadn't said the L-word. Will didn't love her. He was attracted to her, yes, and he'd been honest about it. He'd also been honest enough *not* to have told her that he loved her, just to get her into bed.

So tonight was a gift.

Tomorrow, the lifeswap would be over. Will would walk out of her life, go back to his world. And she'd go on with her plans—do her MBA, make partner, and prove to everyone in the firm that she belonged.

But tonight…tonight, he was hers. To have and to hold.

And as she drifted to sleep in his arms, she was smiling.

CHAPTER FOURTEEN

THE NEXT morning, Amanda woke to find Will sprawled across most of the bed. By contrast, she had most of the sheet she'd substituted for her duvet during the hot weather—there was only one corner of the sheet draped over Will's hips.

Naked, he was beautiful. His pectoral muscles were perfectly defined, his stomach was washboard flat and his thighs were strong. She could tell by his regular breathing that he was still asleep, and she couldn't resist sliding her hand under the sheet to stroke his hipbone.

A man to die for. A man who'd made love to her so thoroughly last night that the endorphins were still fizzing round her system this morning. And that sculptured body wasn't due to working out at the gym, it was from his lifestyle.

Her smile faded and she paused with her hand still resting on his hip. A lifestyle so far away from her own. This wasn't going to work, so she needed to end it now before she was in too deep. Before she got *really* hurt.

'Right a bit,' a sultry voice murmured in her ear.

She snatched her hand away, her face burning with embarrassment. 'How long have you been awake?'

'Long enough.'

'Why didn't you say anything?'

'Because I was enjoying myself.' He gave her a sidelong look. 'I like it when you touch me, Amanda.' He propped himself up on one elbow and leaned over to kiss her lightly. 'Don't stop,' he whispered.

'I…we can't. I have to be in the office. And you hate the rush hour.'

'So we need to save some time? Hmmm.'

Before she guessed his intentions, he'd climbed out of bed, whipped the sheet away, scooped her into his arms and carried her into the bathroom.

'What are you doing?' she asked.

'Saving time.' He kissed her shoulder. 'We're going to have a shower together.'

Just as well he was carrying her, as the idea made her knees buckle.

'Why do you keep picking me up?' she asked.

'Because I can.' He laughed, and let her slide down his body until her feet touched the floor again. 'You're little and cute and it brings out the caveman in me.'

She hadn't seen him as a caveman—more as a pirate, dark and dangerous and incredibly desirable.

He switched on the shower, stepped inside, and beckoned to her. When she didn't move, he shrugged, walked out of the shower—trailing water everywhere—and hauled her in with him.

'Will! We can't—'

'Yes, we can,' he cut in, and poured shower gel on to his palm. He gave her the sexiest smile she'd ever seen, then worked the gel into a lather, spun her round so her back was towards him, and stroked lather on to her skin. Stroked from the nape of her neck across her shoulders, then down to the base of her spine and fluttering up her sides.

Oh-h-h.

And then he turned her to face him again, lathering across her collarbones and down her sides to her ribcage; he circled her navel, teasing and inciting her until she was near the point of begging him to touch her breasts.

As if he could read her mind, he did so, cupping them and rubbing the pads of his thumbs over her nipples.

'You're exquisite,' he breathed, 'and I think this is torturing me more than it's teasing you.' He dropped to his knees and worked on lathering her legs, working from her feet to her ankles to her calves to her knees. When he reached her thighs and stroked them apart, she was shivering with need. And when he touched the tip of his tongue to her sex, she nearly screamed.

He brought her nearer and nearer to the edge, until her hands were tangled in his hair and she was actually whimpering.

Then in one lithe movement he stood up, lifted her and supported her weight against the wall; the coldness of the tiles made her gasp and arch towards him so her body was pressed against his.

'Wrap your legs round my waist,' he told her huskily. 'It'll balance us better.'

And then he entered her.

Amanda wasn't prepared for how he made her feel. With the water streaming down over her and his body pushing into hers, it was astonishing, as if she were in the middle of a thunderstorm, with lightning flashing every time he pushed deep inside her and the thunder being the beating of her heart.

She cried out as her climax hit her. Will supported her weight, holding her close until the aftershocks had died away, then set her down on her feet.

Then it was her turn to wash him. Such an *intimate* task. But she enjoyed the feeling of his muscles beneath her fingers, exploring him and finding out where he was ticklish and what made him hiss with pleasure.

Just as she was about to return the favour—use her mouth to drive him as crazy as he'd driven her—he drew her to her feet.

'We,' he said huskily, 'are going to be late. And although I'd love to spend the entire day in bed with you, you'd hate me for it.'

'Hate you?' she asked, mystified.

'Because it'd mean throwing a sickie. Which I'd guess is very much against your principles.'

She closed her eyes. 'Yeah.'

'Hey...' he kissed her, slow and lingering '...we have time. Later.' He stroked her face. 'Have I told you how incredible you are?'

She couldn't speak.

'Feel.' He took her hand and placed it over his heart. 'You actually make my heart miss beats.'

'Now you're flannelling me.'

He shook his head. 'Honest truth. Race you to getting dressed.' He turned off the shower. 'Amanda.' His voice grew husky. *'Amazing.'*

She didn't feel quite so amazing when she'd finished dressing, walked into the kitchen and registered just how crumpled Will's suit was. Her own would have to go to the dry cleaner's, she thought wryly.

'Coffee,' he said, pushing the mug over towards her.

'Thanks. I, um, I'm sorry about your suit.'

'I'm not.' His eyes were still that sultry, sexy, storm-gold colour. 'And before you start panicking that people are going to notice, they won't.'

She wasn't so sure. Ed and his cronies were always the first to pick up the faintest hint of a scandal. They'd guess straight away that she and Will had had a mad affair.

'Don't worry,' he said. 'Everything's going to be fine.'

'How do you know that?'

'I just do.' He picked up her hand and kissed each finger in turn. 'You worry too much.'

All the same, she couldn't shift the uneasiness—despite the fact that Will held her hand all the way to the Tube station. It was already too much of a squash for them to get a seat next to each other, and Will, being Will, insisted that she should be the one to sit down.

'I'm taller than you are,' he reminded her. 'It's not such a stretch for me to hang on to the bar.'

She could hardly argue with that.

More and more people got onto the train, and in the end she could barely see Will. At their stop, he waited for her outside the train; they walked in near silence to her office.

For the first time ever, Amanda found that work actually dragged. The morning was full of time-consuming, annoyingly trivial things that needed to be sorted out. A phone call from Rhiannon meant that she'd be out at the client's tomorrow morning, sorting out some glitches in the audit. Yet, at the same time, the minutes seemed to rush by. The last few minutes before Will would be leaving London.

And then it was three o'clock.

The time they'd agreed to leave the office so Will wouldn't have too much of a nightmare journey back to Cambridge.

He hadn't actually packed yet. Because they'd been otherwise oc- cupied that morning, Amanda thought with a flash of shame. But it only took him ten minutes—and half of that involved changing back into his scruffy jeans.

'So. The end of Dee's lifeswap project.'

'Was it as bad as you thought, in my world?'

'Put it this way, I wouldn't swap it for mine,' he admitted. 'Though there were some high points. One or two *really* spectacular ones.' He brushed his mouth against hers. 'Come home with me for the weekend, Amanda.'

It was tempting. So, so tempting.

A weekend of pottering around the garden and walking by the river on Sunday afternoon.

A weekend of Will's fabulous cooking.

A weekend of making love and exploring each other—a whole weekend with the sexy pirate who'd hauled her into the shower and made love to her until she'd forgotten the world.

So tempting.

But she didn't belong in the Fens, and she knew it. She was a city girl. If he tempted her there, she'd end up like her mother, bitter and resentful, and everything they'd shared would be like ashes in her mouth. 'I can't,' she whispered. 'I need to sort something out at a client's tomorrow.'

'So where do we go from here?' he asked softly.

Crunch time. She'd been thinking about it all day. Will and his…*we have time*. *Later*. Except that was then and this was the real world. 'I think it's best that we end it now. Before either of us gets hurt.'

He raised an eyebrow. 'Is that what you really want? Or are you just scared to take a risk?'

She didn't rise to the bait. 'We're too different. There isn't enough crossover between us for this to work.'

'Ever heard the saying "where there's a will there's a way"? I'm good at fixing things.'

She shook her head. 'I don't need fixing.'

'Okay. If you won't come home with me, I'll ring Fliss and ask her to take care of Sunny for a bit longer, change my train ticket, and stay with you for the weekend. The gardens can wait.'

He'd put her before his business? But it wasn't just his business, was it? 'That's not fair—and, anyway, Dee's due home tonight.' She dragged in a breath. Neither of them had said they loved each other. It was the right time to call a halt. Before she lost her heart completely. 'Will, a clean break's better.'

'So this is goodbye, not *au revoir*?'

She nodded. 'This is goodbye.'

He looked at her. 'The lady's not for turning, eh?' he asked wryly. 'Well—goodbye, then. Good luck with the MBA. And you deserve to make partner at a terrifyingly young age.'

'Good luck with the designing. And think about entering Chelsea. I think you'd be up for a gold.'

'Maybe.'

For a moment, she thought he was going to kiss her. Then he picked up his case and walked out of the door. Out of her life.

It was all over.

'I thought Will was supposed to teach you to slow down a bit?' Dee asked, almost a week later. 'If anything, you're working even harder.'

Hard enough not to miss him. That was the idea. She needed to work until she was too tired to think about him. Too tired to remember how it felt to sleep in his arms. Too tired to pick up the phone and call him and admit how much she wanted him. 'I'm fine,' Amanda lied. 'Busy time at work. Year ends, and all that.'

Dee scoffed. 'The tax year ends in April.'

'But a company's year end doesn't necessarily end in April. Some end in July. Anyway, I need to start preparing for my MBA.'

'You're heading for a breakdown, if you keep up this pace,' Dee warned.

'I'm fine,' Amanda insisted. Or she would be if she could get Will's face out of her head.

'So Fliss decided to bring in the big guns, hmm?' Will asked, giving his aunt a hug.

'Something like that. Will, she's worried about you. She says you're working like a demon.'

'Just making the most of the light evenings. The nights are starting to pull in already,' Will said.

'Hmmm. Even Sunny looks as if she's moping.' Helen made a

fuss of the dog. 'It's this girl, isn't it? The one you did that lifeswap thing with.'

Will grimaced. 'Helen, you're the nearest I have to a mother—' a hell of a lot more so than his own was '—but I don't want to talk about it. Even to you.'

'Why don't you just go and see her? Talk to her?' Helen asked.

'Because she made it clear she isn't interested.' He placed a mug of coffee in front of her. 'And I'm not going to beg.'

Helen rolled her eyes. 'Male pride. Tell me—what use is it? You're clearly eating your heart out over her. Go and see her. What have you got to lose?'

Will shrugged. 'We're from different worlds. She'd hate it here and I can't live in London. I can't *breathe* in London.'

Helen frowned. 'She does know you live in Cambridge, doesn't she? You did come clean?'

He didn't answer; merely turned his own mug of coffee round and round on the table.

'Oh, Will. For someone so clever, you can be such a dope.' She reached over to ruffle his hair. 'I can understand the Fens aren't everyone's cup of tea. But if she's a city girl, she'd be able to settle here in Cambridge. There's a solution staring you right in the face. But if you're intent on doing this stupid male pride thing...'

'Helen, she's *driven*. Even more so than my parents. And I spent too much of my childhood coming second to their career. I don't want to come second to hers.'

'Who's to say you will?' Helen asked.

'She's studying for an MBA, part time. Between that and her job, she doesn't have any spare time.'

'And how long is this for—a couple of years?' At his nod, she smiled. 'What's a couple of years, in the whole of a lifetime?'

'I suppose,' Will said.

'Go and see her. Don't let your pride get in the way. If you want her, fight for her,' Helen advised.

'Mmm.'

'Before,' she said quietly, 'it's too late.'

It took Will four days to swallow his pride. He considered ringing Amanda first; then again, she was stubborn enough to refuse to see him. If he drove up and knocked on her front door, she'd have to talk to him.

The seeds they'd planted together had grown into sturdy little seedlings. He gathered up four of the pots she'd planted, placed them carefully in a box in the back of his car, then made a fuss of Sunny and checked that she had plenty of water. 'You can't come with me, this time,' he told the dog gently. 'She's not allowed to have dogs in her flat. But hopefully…' Hopefully she'd listen to him. Agree to give them a chance.

But when he knocked on the door, Dee answered.

'Hello! I didn't know you were coming tonight.'

'Just passing. How's the pilot tape?' he asked.

'I'm waiting to hear from Saskia's boss. Keep your fingers crossed for me.' She gave him a hug. 'You were a star. Thanks. I couldn't have done it without you.'

'No worries. Um, is Amanda in?'

Dee shook her head. 'Working.'

'What, at this time of night?' he asked, shocked. He'd been so sure she'd be home.

'Tell me about it. I think she's in the library, preparing something for her MBA.' Dee sighed. 'She works too hard. Like you said on the tape, she needs to learn to slow down and breathe, let alone smell the roses. I have no idea what time she's going to be back.'

Will shrugged. 'I brought her these—they're the ones she planted.' He handed the box to Dee.

'Look, can I get you a cup of coffee, or something?'

'No, it's okay. Thanks for the offer, but I was just passing. Really.'

'I could ring her mobile?' Dee offered.

Will shook his head. There was no point. Because finding her working at this time of night told him that this was what life would always be like with Amanda—he'd always come second to her career, just as he had to his parents'. Exactly as he'd told Helen. 'I can't really stay. I need to get home for Sunny.'

'Well, it was nice to see you. I'll give her the plants,' Dee said.

'Thanks.'

And he tried to ignore the regret seeping through him as he drove home. Amanda was right. It was never going to work.

So how come he felt as if his life had just turned monochrome?

* * *

When Amanda finally came in, an hour later, Dee was curled up with a magazine. 'Hey. I wondered if you were coming home tonight!'

'I told you I was going to be late,' Amanda reminded her.

'Will stopped by.'

'Will?' Amanda's spine tingled. She'd had no idea he was going to call in. He hadn't phoned her once since he'd left London. No text, no email, nothing. No contact whatsoever. And she'd told herself she was an idiot for hoping he'd ignore her words about a clean break. 'Why?'

'Just passing. He dropped off some plants—something about them being the seeds you'd planted?'

'Oh.' Amanda swallowed hard.

'He looked nearly as bad as you do,' Dee said thoughtfully. 'Dark shadows under his eyes. I've never seen him like that before.'

'He's probably busy at work,' Amanda said. If he was feeling as miserable and alone as she was, right now, then he should have called her. Or at least waited for her to get back tonight. The fact he hadn't waited…well, that told her everything. He wasn't prepared to wait. Loathed the city. He'd expect her to be the one to make all the compromises: and she couldn't bear the idea of feeling cut off and out of place, as she always had as a child.

'Hmmm,' Dee said. 'I think you're in denial. Both of you. Why don't you go and see him, Mand?'

'Because,' Amanda said crisply, 'there's no point. And if you'll excuse me, I'm going to have a bath.'

And this time, maybe, she wouldn't have flashbacks to the time Will had made love to her in the shower…

CHAPTER FIFTEEN

A FEW weeks later, Amanda was feeling decidedly out of sorts. Maybe it was some sort of summer flu, she thought. Except she didn't know of anyone else who was feeling as grim as this. Besides, she was almost never ill.

But when she couldn't even drink a cup of coffee at her desk, she began to wonder. Especially when she realised that her period was over a week late.

Stress, probably. Nothing more than that.

She couldn't be pregnant. When she and Will had made love, they'd definitely used protection.

But supposing…?

No. Of course not. The chances of contraception not working were pretty low.

Yet the idea wouldn't shift from her head. And she ended up going home via a supermarket she didn't normally use, to buy a test kit. It'd prove once and for all that this whole thing was in her head and she just had some sort of virus.

To Amanda's relief, Dee was out at a journalist's party—a party she'd tried hard to persuade her flatmate to go to, though it really wasn't Amanda's kind of thing at all—and she had the flat to herself. No questions to answer.

She read the instructions, did the test, and waited.

Two minutes, while the second hand ticked slowly, slowly round the dial.

She couldn't be pregnant.

Please don't let her be pregnant.

This really wasn't the right time to fall for a baby…

One blue line. So the test was working. Okay. Now let the other window stay blank.

Please.
Please, please, please.
Fifteen seconds to go.
Tick, tick, tick.
Please, please, pl—
She stared at the test in disbelief. It couldn't be. There had to be some sort of mistake.
But there were two blue lines.
She was pregnant.

It took Amanda a good ten minutes to walk into the kitchen again. She poured herself a glass of water and slumped into a chair. Pregnant. With Will's baby. What the hell was she going to do?

The obvious thing was to tell him. He had a right to know. But this was hardly something she could do on the phone. Supposing he was out? No way could she leave him a message like that on the answering machine. *Hi, Will. It's Amanda. By the way, I'm pregnant with your baby.*

She needed to tell him this face-to-face. Which meant going back to his world.

And then what?

She couldn't have a baby. Not when she was just about to start two years of intensive study. Not when she was at such a crucial point in her career—if she put everything on hold to have a baby, she'd be finished. Just like her mother had been. Everything she'd worked so hard for thrown away. She'd never get another chance—and her juniors would overtake her. She'd lose out. Have to work for people who'd worked for her. Take steps *backward*.

She couldn't do it.

And what made her think she'd be any good as a mother anyway? Not with the role model she'd had, growing up. Supposing Amanda had the baby and then discovered she disliked children as much as her mother did? She'd never really been around children. Not so much as held a baby, because none of her friends had children or wanted them.

Friends? Ha. Who was she trying to kid? She didn't really have friends. She had colleagues. Just like her mother had. And when they'd moved to the country, the bonds of acquaintanceship had snapped.

For the first time, Amanda began to understand how her mother had felt when Amanda had been a child. All these plans, a glittering career before her—and then everything juddering to a halt because of what some people called a 'happy accident'.

There hadn't been anything happy about Amanda's childhood.

Could she really make her own child go through that same misery, the same knowledge that she wasn't wanted and she'd ruined her mother's life?

And her mother was the last person she could discuss this with. There wouldn't be any sympathy, any understanding—just contempt and a demand to know how Amanda could have been so stupid, making exactly the same mistake her mother had done. Pregnant before she'd reached the top. A career break that would give everyone the chance to rush past her. Moving out to the country when the family budget hadn't been able to stretch back to London—and then being stuck because house prices in London had rocketed so much faster than the rest of the country that they couldn't afford to move back to the city.

Trapped.

And alone.

'What the hell am I going to do?' Amanda whispered.

There was one solution. One obvious solution.

But she was going to have to sleep on this one.

Luckily Amanda's colleagues were used to her being quiet in the office, so nobody made any comments over the next few days. Nobody noticed that she'd stopped drinking coffee, either; the summer had blossomed into a heatwave, so everyone was opting for chilled drinks. And Dee, who was finding it too sticky and airless to sleep properly at night, accepted Amanda's explanation that it was the same for her.

Night after night, Amanda lay awake and thought about it. Keep the baby—or stop everything now. It was her body, her choice…

Except it wasn't just her choice, was it?

Every time she thought about it, a little bit more of her said she couldn't go through with it. And as the week went by, she began to realise that she didn't have to follow her mother's path. She wasn't her mother. It didn't have to be the same for her. She wouldn't bring up her child in the same way.

She could have it all.

If she was brave enough.

And then at last it was Saturday morning. Amanda supposed she ought to call Will first, but then what would she say? 'I need to talk to you.' He'd ask why. And it wasn't a conversation she wanted to have on the phone. No, best just to turn up and tell him.

She left early and was parked outside the cottage at half past eight. Will's battered estate car wasn't there; another car was in its place. She frowned. Maybe he had friends staying and his car wasn't there because he was at the garden centre or at a client's.

There was only one way to find out.

She ignored the adrenalin prickling at the back of her neck, climbed out of the car and knocked on the door.

It was a while before the door opened and a man she didn't recognise leaned against the doorjamb. 'Can I help you?' he asked.

'I was looking for Will,' she said.

'Will?'

This must be the man's idea of a joke—pretending that he had no idea who Will was. Of *course* he knew. He was in Will's house, wasn't he?

'Will Daynes,' she said.

He shook his head and smiled ruefully at her. 'Sorry, love. I think you've got the wrong place.'

No, no, no. There had to be some mistake. She'd spent a whole week here. She hadn't got the wrong place—she *knew* she hadn't.

A woman came up behind him and slid her arms round his waist. 'Did I hear you say Daynes?' she asked.

Amanda felt sick. 'Yes.'

'Mr Daynes owns the cottage—he might be at the garden centre. We collected the key from him there last Saturday afternoon, remember, love?' she said to the man.

The words sank in: *collected the key from him.* 'You're on holiday here?' she asked.

The woman smiled. 'Some of our friends stayed here last year and recommended it to us. It's one of the nicest holiday cottages we've stayed in.'

Holiday cottage?

The full ramifications slammed into her. Will had lied to her. He'd made her believe this was his home and he'd *lied* to her.

'I'm sorry to have disturbed your holiday,' she said.

'You haven't disturbed us. We're packing to go home,' the woman said.

'It'll be a shame to leave here. It's a lovely part of the world and the kids adored it,' the man added.

Kids.

Oh, God. If Will had lied to her about where he lived, had he lied to her about being single, too? Was he married? Did he have children? Had she made the most stupid mistake of her life? Was she pregnant by a married man whose wife 'didn't understand him'?

'Are you all right, love?' the woman asked.

'Yes—it's this heat. Takes it out of you,' Amanda said swiftly.

'Can I get you a glass of water or something?' the woman asked, still looking concerned.

A complete stranger, and yet she'd been kind. It was enough to make Amanda want to cry.

Hormones. And she needed them back under control. Right now. 'No, no, I'm fine. Glad you enjoyed your holiday.' She forced a smile to her face and got back into the car.

The garden centre. When she'd arrived here on the Saturday morning, Will had said something about a staff meeting at the garden centre. Or had he lied about that, too?

She'd still tell him about the baby, because he had a right to know. But that was as far as it went. This baby was hers—they didn't need a lying, cheating rat like Will Daynes in their lives.

She drove to the garden centre, scrubbing the tears from her face with the back of her hand. She was *not* going to cry over Will Daynes. This was just her hormones going haywire, that was all.

The first person she saw in green overalls was a young lad she didn't remember from her visits to the garden centre. 'Excuse me, is Mr Daynes in, please?'

The young lad frowned. 'I'm not sure, I'll just check—who shall I tell him it is?'

'It's personal.' She shook her head. 'Never mind. I know where his office is.' She stomped through the corridor and slammed the door open.

But the man sitting behind the desk wasn't Will. He was a good twenty years older than Will, though she could see a resemblance in those beautiful eyes and the shape of his face. And in the same second of realisation she heard barking.

A dog.

More than one dog.

Remembering the Alsatian from her childhood, she flinched back against the wall.

'You two, sit down and be quiet. Now,' the man ordered, and the two dogs slunk back to their position behind his desk, looking sheepish. Then he turned to Amanda. 'Can I help you?'

'I was looking for Will…' To her horror, she heard her voice quiver and felt tears welling up.

The man came round to her side of the desk and gently shepherded her into a chair. 'Sit down, love. You look all in. Wait there, and I'll get you a glass of water. The collies won't hurt you, though they might try to herd you on to a chair.'

He was joking about the latter.

She hoped.

He fixed them with a stern look. 'Charlie, Susie—*stay.*'

Before she could protest, he disappeared, and came back with a glass of water. 'I'm Martin Daynes, Will's uncle,' he said.

The one Will really liked. *The original Sixties child.* The one who'd given him his love of music. 'You own the garden centre?' she asked.

'Yes.'

'And the cottage?'

He winced. 'Um, yes.'

'I'm Amanda Neave,' she said quietly.

He nodded. 'I should've guessed.'

'Will *lied* to me.' She dragged in a breath. 'About everything.'

Martin sighed. 'Oh, love. I'm sorry. I knew this was a bad idea right from the start.'

'The lifeswap thing?' A tall, pretty woman walked into the room and held her hand out to Amanda. 'Hello. I'm Helen, Will's aunt.'

Amanda was too distraught to take Helen's hand. 'He lied to me,' she repeated.

'Not out of ill intentions. He's not like that.' Helen perched on the edge of Martin's desk. 'Will's very family oriented.'

Worse and worse. 'So he's married?' Amanda dug her nails into her palm.

'No. He's single,' Martin said. 'And he hasn't been seeing anyone since—*ow*.'

Helen had clearly poked him with a pen to shut him up. And before Amanda could ask what Martin meant, Helen said, 'He did the lifeswap thing to help his sister's best friend, because she needed a country boy for her project.'

A foil to the city chick. 'Dee. My flatmate,' Amanda said tonelessly.

Helen nodded. 'And also for me, so I could get Martin to take a week's break—you wouldn't believe how hard it is to persuade some people to take a holiday.' Then she put her hand over her mouth and her eyes widened. 'Whoops. Sorry, I wasn't being rude about you.'

'It's okay. I know what people think of me. Control freak, workaholic…Whatever.' Amanda lifted her chin. 'So Will isn't a garden designer?'

'Oh, he is,' Martin reassured her. 'And he's brilliant. But he likes to do things his way. Which is why he works for himself, not for me. He kept an eye on the place while we were away for the week, but he can't stand being stuck in an office.'

So he'd been truthful about that part.

'And he doesn't live in the Fens.' It was a statement rather than a question.

Helen frowned. 'He said he was going to come clean and tell you the truth about where he lived. Didn't he come and see you?'

Amanda nodded. And he'd brought her the sunflowers they'd planted together. 'I wasn't there.'

'You were working late,' Helen guessed. 'Stupid boy. Why didn't he wait for you to come home?' She rolled her eyes. 'Men! Mind you, in some respects I'm not surprised.'

'Why?' Amanda asked.

Helen shook her head. 'I think he should be the one to explain that. But if he doesn't, ask him about his parents.'

His parents? 'He didn't say much about them,' Amanda said. 'Though he talked about you both.'

Martin and Helen exchanged a glance.

'I did get the impression his parents weren't pleased he turned down an unconditional place at Oxford.'

'He told you about *that*?' Helen asked.

Amanda frowned. 'It's not something he talks about?'

'Almost never. The fact he told you…' Helen shook her head in exasperation. 'I could strangle him for being so dense. I think you two need to talk. Sooner, rather than later. He's not far away— he lives in Cambridge.'

No wonder he'd known so much about the city. And that explained why they'd seemed to recognise him in the bakery and why he'd parked in a side road instead of a public car park before she reminded him it was a permit-parking area.

The area for which he possessed a permit, she'd guess.

'I'm sorry I disturbed you,' Amanda said, standing up.

'You're not disturbing us—and you're not a nuisance, either, before you suggest it,' Helen said. Her eyes narrowed. 'You look as if you've been crying, love.'

Tears never seemed far from the surface at the moment. 'I'm all right,' Amanda said.

'No, you're not. I'll ring him and get him to drive over here,' Martin said.

Amanda shook her head. She really didn't want an audience when she spoke to Will—especially people who were as kind and concerned as Martin and Helen. What would they say if they knew they could be a great-aunt and great-uncle in a few months' time? 'I'll be fine.'

'Then why don't I drive you over to his place?' Martin suggested.

Helen laid her hand on his arm. 'I think Amanda might need to see Will on her own, love.'

Amanda felt her eyes widen. Surely Helen hadn't guessed? It was really early days—no way were there any physical signs.

But Martin was still frowning. 'You know what Cambridge is like. It's a nightmare to park.'

Helen fished a piece of paper out of the mess on Martin's desk and scribbled down an address and a rough map. 'It's really easy to find. Just park outside his house. And he can either sort out a permit or pay your parking ticket, whichever you prefer.'

'At the moment,' Amanda said, 'I think I want to strangle him for lying to me.'

'Hear him out,' Helen advised. 'He's a good man. And his heart's definitely in the right place.' She smiled. 'Good luck, love. It'll all work out. Just talk to him.'

Yeah. Though everything she'd planned to say…it had changed. Will hadn't been honest with her during the lifeswap. How could she trust him to be honest with her now?

CHAPTER SIXTEEN

AMANDA DROVE to Cambridge, still with no idea about what she was going to say, how she was going to tell Will that she was pregnant with his baby. Since Martin and Helen's revelations, everything seemed to be topsy-turvy and she really didn't have a clue what she was doing any more.

She parked on the street and then walked down the road, counting up the numbers until she reached Will's house. Though even without the house number she could've guessed which one was his: a turn-of-the-century terraced house, painted cream, with original sash windows and a door painted a bright sky blue. There was a low brick wall around the pocket-handkerchief-sized front garden and a wrought-iron gate. The plants were a riot of colour, old-fashioned cottage garden plants like the ones he'd shown her at the nursery: delphiniums, foxgloves, love-in-a-mist and lavender, along with other plants she didn't recognise. And the little lilac-coloured rain daisies he'd told her were his favourite—right now they were wide open in honour of the heatwave.

The windows at the top were open, so it looked as if Will was home.

Feeling sick, she opened the gate and walked down the path. She stood there for two whole minutes before she nerved herself to use the polished brass knocker.

There was a soft woof, and then she saw a silhouette behind the frosted glass of the door. Her heart was beating so hard, so fast, she was sure the whole of Cambridge could hear it.

The door opened—and there he was. Will. Wearing only a pair of faded cut-off jeans, frayed round the edges. His hair was wild, he clearly hadn't shaved that morning, and he looked absolutely edible.

As well as very shocked to see her. Clearly his aunt and uncle hadn't called him to warn him she was on her way. She wasn't sure whether that was a good sign or a bad omen.

'Hello, Will,' she said, trying her best to sound cool and calm and collected—even though right now she was in turmoil. She wanted to scream at him for being a liar and making such a fool out of her, but at the same time her body was running riot and ignoring her mind. Remembering what it felt like to touch him. Remembering what it felt like to be touched by him. And how she wanted him to hold her.

'Amanda? What are you doing here?'

'We need to talk.'

He sucked in a breath. 'Oh, hell. You know.'

No way was she making this easy for him. Not after the way he'd lied to her. 'Know what?' she asked, wanting to hear him admit it.

'About the lifeswap thing. That I wasn't completely straight with you about it.' He raked a hand through his hair. 'This wasn't how things were meant to… Look, you'd better come in.'

The interior of the terraced house was nothing like the cottage in the Fens. This felt like *home*. The entrance hall was painted a deep sand colour, the stairs were stripped and varnished, and there was a gorgeous landscape picture hanging on the wall—the kind of painting she'd expected Will to own.

He bypassed the door at the front of the hall and ushered her through to what was clearly the living room. 'Take a seat. I'll make us a drink.'

Again, the room seemed to fit him, warm and vibrant—not like the neutral, cool colours in the Fenland cottage. The walls were a rich red, and a sky-blue fringed silk rug was flung casually onto a stripped and varnished wooden floor. There were pictures clustered on the mantelpiece above the cast-iron fireplace—one of Sunny, one of Fliss in a wedding dress and Will looking amazing in top hat and tails, a couple of Martin and Helen, and one of Fliss in graduation robes with Will making bunny ears behind her head.

Family oriented. Exactly what Helen had said about him. Though there were no pictures of anyone who could be his parents, she noticed. Was he that estranged from them?

The cushions on one of the deep plush chairs appeared to be

covered in dog hair—clearly Sunny's chair—and the bookshelves on either side of the chimney breast were crammed to bursting. Gardening books? Novels? Unable to resist browsing, she discovered an eclectic collection of poetry and novels and horticultural texts, all well thumbed. She'd known that Will was well read—this just confirmed it.

There was a pile of papers on the coffee table; the topmost one looked like a rough design for a garden. She was about to reach out for it when a soft nudge at the side of her knee made her jump: Sunny. Gingerly, she stroked the top of the spaniel's head; apparently satisfied, Sunny bounced on to the chair covered with dog hair and settled down with her nose on her paws.

Yes, this was definitely Will's home. Untidy—and comfortable.

For a second, she wondered what it would be like to call this place home. To come back from the city and see Will sketching a design or messing about with a mood board. To walk in and smell the scent of a good meal being cooked, with ingredients picked from their garden. To see their child playing ball in the garden with Sunny…

But this wasn't her home. She didn't fit Will's life. And she still hadn't told him about the baby.

She returned to her chair and waited; a moment later, Will came in with two mugs of coffee and handed one to her.

He'd pulled on a crumpled T-shirt, she noticed. Though he was still barefoot, like a pirate, and his hair was still a mess, curling everywhere in a way that made her want to run her fingers through it.

Coffee. Um. She really couldn't drink this. But without telling him why… She just hoped he'd think she was too hot for coffee, or something like that, and put the mug beside her on the floor.

Time for the reckoning. 'You lied to me, Will. About the cottage, about your job—about everything.'

He leaned back against the sofa and balanced the side of one foot on his knee. Though she wasn't fooled by his apparent calm; his face looked strained. Guilty. As if he regretted what he'd done.

But what did he regret? Lying to her or making love to her?

'I'm sorry, Amanda. I didn't do it to make you feel like a fool. It was to play up the differences between us for the lifeswap thing.'

'You still lied to me. You're not the honourable man I thought you were.' She felt her hands bunching into fists. 'I'm so *angry* with you, Will.' And confused. And miserable. And her hormones were running riot, now she'd seen him again. She didn't know whether she wanted to kill him or kiss him. Just as well she was sitting in a chair on the opposite side of the room rather than next to him on the sofa.

'If it makes you feel any better, I hate myself for lying to you, too. But what else could I have done?' His eyes were clear green, glittering with a mixture of guilt and pain. 'I never meant to hurt you, Amanda.'

'But you have.' He hadn't trusted her with the truth. So how could she trust him?

'And I'm sorry for that. Truly sorry.' He swallowed hard. 'I wanted to help Dee. She's my sister's best friend—practically family. And it was my chance to give something back to Martin. He and Helen brought me up.'

Helen had told her to ask him about his parents if he didn't tell her. It sounded as if this was the key to Will. But could she trust him enough to tell her the truth? 'Why?' she asked quietly. 'Are your parents…?' No, she couldn't ask him that. If his parents had been killed in an accident or something, asking him about it would rip his scars wide open.

As if he'd guessed what she'd been about to ask, he said, 'No, they're alive. Probably—' he glanced at his watch '—asleep. In Tokyo or New York or somewhere.'

'You don't know where they are?' Despite her difficult relationship with her own parents, she was shocked that he could be so isolated from his.

He shrugged. 'If I need to know, I can ask their secretary for a schedule.'

'So you're not on good terms with them, then?'

'Not on bad terms, either.'

She frowned. 'I'm not with you.'

'I don't really have a relationship with my parents,' he said. 'I don't see them very often. We've never been close.'

She could appreciate that one—it was how things were with her own parents. But *she*'d been a mistake. 'You're the youngest.' His parents must have planned to have at least one child—having two accidental pregnancies was pretty unlikely. 'And surely they were delighted to have a son and heir?'

He quickly disillusioned her. 'They couldn't wait to ship me off to boarding school. Martin and Helen couldn't have children, so they more or less claimed Fliss and me in the summer holidays.' He shrugged. 'Otherwise, my parents would've probably engaged a string of nannies or something to look after us. Which is pretty much what they did when we weren't old enough to go to boarding school.'

Why on earth didn't his parents have time for him?

The question must have been written all over her face because he said, 'They're merchant bankers. Rather high up in their respective companies. And they have a very, very, *very* busy schedule.'

Uh-oh. Finance. His parents came from her world. Probably worked the kind of long hours that she did. Suddenly, it fell into place—why Will loathed London so much. And why he hadn't waited for her. He'd thought she was in the same mould as his parents were and he'd always come second to her job, the way he'd come second to theirs. 'I'm sorry.'

'Not your fault.'

'So they expected you to follow in their footsteps.' Get a First at Oxford and follow them into finance. Pretty much what he'd said to her before—he could have ended up doing a job like hers. 'Except you followed in Martin's.'

He nodded. 'My first job was a holiday job in the garden centre. Martin taught me everything I know about plants. And he backed me when I decided to study horticulture. Encouraged me to follow my heart and do what I really loved. So doing the lifeswap thing for Dee was a way of paying him back. Getting him some publicity for the garden centre—publicity he needs.'

'Because he's a specialist and he's finding it hard to compete with the big chains?'

'Exactly.'

'So your garden design…'

'That bit was true. But it's for me, not for Martin, and it's full time. I've made enough of a name that I can pick and choose my clients.' He shrugged. 'Will Daynes, landscaper to the rich and famous.'

'A modern-day Capability Brown.'

He raised an eyebrow. 'Been reading up?'

He'd caught her out—and he knew it, because his eyes crinkled at the corners. 'I'd like to think my work will be remembered in the same way in years to come. Sometimes I think I've sold out—but on the other hand it pays me well enough so I can do smaller gardens for fun. Help people who have a dream, but who don't know where to start making it come true—and who can't afford to buy mature plants.'

'Like the woman with the tiny courtyard who came to the garden centre for advice.'

'Yup.' He paused. 'So now you know the truth.'

'All of it?' She needed to know. 'Did you lie to me in London?'

'Just to get you into bed?' He shook his head. 'Of course not. And I'm not in a relationship with anyone else.'

He wasn't in a relationship with her, either.

Except…

She had to tell him. Tell him *now*. 'As you've brought the subject up…I'm here because you need to know something.' She swallowed. Why was this so hard? It was the kind of news most people would consider 'good'. Though she wasn't his partner and he had issues with his parents, so having a child of his own might not be on his agenda.

Not that she was planning for him to be a big part of the baby's life. This was her mistake, and she'd deal with it.

'Amanda?' he prompted.

There was no easy way to tell him. Might as well just tell him straight. 'I'm pregnant.'

He stared at her. 'Pregnant?'

At least he hadn't asked her if it was his. One small mercy. 'Don't worry, I'm not expecting anything from you. I'm perfectly able to support a child by myself.'

'You're pregnant,' he repeated.

'I just thought you had a right to know. And it's not the kind of thing you can say on the phone or in an email.'

He shook his head as if trying to clear it. 'You're *pregnant*.'

He looked shell-shocked. Well, that made two of them. Though she'd had the best part of a week to get used to the idea.

Then his face changed. The strain vanished—replaced by a smile of sheer joy. 'You're pregnant,' he breathed in wonder. 'We're having a baby.'

'I'm having a baby,' she corrected.

'You're having *my* baby. Our baby.' The silver was back in his eyes. 'When?'

She hadn't exactly thought about that. 'I did a test earlier this week.'

'We're going to have a baby.'

'You're not listening to me, Will. This is *my* baby.'

The corner of his mouth quirked. 'You don't make a baby on your own, Amanda. It takes two. And in this case, that means you and me. Our baby. And I'm going to look after you.'

She shook her head. 'No way. That's what happened to my mother.'

Amanda's mother. She hadn't said much about her parents—but the little she had told him made Will think that hers were as bad as his. They hadn't tried to help her get over her fear of dogs. When she'd stung herself on those nettles, she'd admitted she wasn't used to people making a fuss over her. And if nobody had paid her much attention as a child…no wonder she was reserved with people now. Because nobody had ever taught her how to make friends. 'What happened to your mother?' he asked, his voice gentle.

'She got pregnant with me. She was meant to be a high flyer. Except…she had me.'

He frowned. 'There are such things as career breaks.'

'Not back then. And when I was old enough for her to go back to work, she was way behind everyone else. They'd all moved on.' Her face tightened. 'And we couldn't afford to move back to London anyway. So she was still trapped—trapped in a place she hated.'

Finally, he understood why she was driven. Because of her mother's disappointment. 'So you became a high flyer for her. To make it up to her.'

A muscle twitched in her face. 'Don't be ridiculous. I did it for me.'

Talk about in denial.

He'd just bet Amanda hated the country because she associated it with her mother being miserable and had convinced herself she'd feel the same. The middle of the Fens was probably too remote for her, admittedly, but Cambridge was another matter. Helen's words

echoed in his ears: *There's a solution staring you right in the face.*
Of course there was. Cambridge. A city with lots of green spaces
and gardens. A place that would work for both of them.

'Have you told your mother about the baby?' Will asked.

Amanda shook her head. 'You're the only one who knows.'

And he could imagine how much it had cost her to tell him.

Ah, hell. He couldn't stay away from her any longer. He scooped
her out of the chair, sat down in her place, and settled her on his lap.

'Will, what are you—?' she began.

'You've just told me that you're expecting my baby.' He placed
one hand gently over her abdomen. 'Do you really think I'm going
to stay on the other side of the room rather than be close to you?'

'I…' She shrugged.

'That's not who I am.' He took a deep breath. 'Look, the
baby…this changes everything. This isn't just about you and me any
more. We're going to have a baby. I had a rough childhood, apart
from Martin and Helen. I don't think yours was much better. And
that's not going to be the case for our baby.'

'My baby,' she said stubbornly.

'*Our* baby,' he insisted. 'And I'm even more stubborn than you
are, so don't argue, Amanda. You'll lose.'

She said nothing, just glared at him.

Lord, he wanted to kiss that scowl away. But he knew they needed
to sort this out properly first. Amanda needed to know things with
her head before she could trust her heart. 'I know part of the problem
is that you work in London and you thought I lived in the middle of
nowhere. But it's not the real situation. I live in a city.'

'Cambridge isn't London.'

'No. Actually, it's the best of both worlds. I'll still have a decent garden and be able to hear birdsong in the morning, and
you're in commuting distance of London.'

Her mouth thinned. 'So I'm going to be the one making all the
compromises.'

'It's not a compromise. You'll still be doing the job you love,
and I'll be doing mine. Actually, the more I think about it, you
don't even have to commute. Your firm has a branch in Cambridge.
What's to stop you getting a transfer and a partnership here?'

'With a baby?' She stared at him in seeming disbelief. '*And* I'm going to have to give up my MBA. How can I study when I'm having a baby?'

Was Amanda like her mother? Was she seeing a baby as an obstacle to her career rather than a tiny miracle that would enrich her life? 'Are you thinking about having a termination?' he asked, not sure he wanted to hear the answer.

'I don't know.' She dragged in a breath. 'Right now everything seems a mess and a muddle.'

'And you think your career plans have all gone down the plughole.'

'Of course they have.'

'Actually, they haven't.' He stroked her face. 'Think about it. You'll need to take some time off—even *you* can't make notes on a lecture while you're in labour—but there's no reason why you can't still do your MBA.'

'How?'

'You're not doing this on your own.' He tucked a tendril of hair behind her ear. 'This is my baby too. I'll be supporting you.'

'On weekends?'

He rolled his eyes. 'I have no intention of being a weekend father. I'm going to be a full-time father.'

She stared at him, eyes wide and full of fear. 'You're going to take me to court for custody?'

'For someone so clever, you can be completely clueless at times.' Pretty much what Helen had said to him: *For someone so clever, you can be such a dope.* He smiled at the memory. 'No. I'm going to live with you.'

She blinked. 'But I live in London. You live here.'

'That's easily solved. Move in with me.'

She shook her head in exasperation. 'As I said, you're expecting me to be the one who has to make all the compromises.'

Put like that, she had a point. Moving in with him was the perfect solution—but it would mean she'd have to give up her flat, change her job. 'Okay. Let's do this another way. I'll sell my house and we'll buy another one. Together.' At her narrowed eyes, he added quietly, 'In London.'

'But you *hate* London. You said you couldn't live anywhere else except the Fens.'

'Cambridgeshire,' he corrected. 'But you're absolutely right. I need to make compromises, too. So I'll learn to live in London.'

She swallowed. 'It won't work. I heard what you said on the tape about feeling trapped.'

'Cabin'd, cribb'd, confin'd?' He smiled. 'Forget it. I was being a bit melodramatic. Pretending I was Macbeth.'

'No, you weren't. You could barely sit still in the office. You kept fiddling with the plants and you were desperate to get out of the building and go for a walk in the nearest park.'

He tried to make a joke of it. 'Rats. Rumbled.'

'You'd feel as trapped in London as I would in the Fens. I grew up in the country, Will. I grew up with everyone watching every single thing I did. I grew up never quite fitting in because my mum was a city girl and didn't want to be part of the village. She never invited people back to our place and people got sick of being the ones doing all the hospitality, so the invitations stopped. I was a nuisance, to everyone. And I don't want to feel like that again.'

'You won't. Because you'll be with me. You fit with me, Amanda.' She'd been brave enough to come here and tell him about the baby. Maybe it was time he was brave enough to tell her something, too. 'I came to London because I missed you. I wanted you back in my life. And I'd rather be caged in London with you than free without you.'

She stared at him, frowning. 'Really?'

'Really.' There was a tiny, tiny spark of something in her face that gave him courage. 'So I'm going to say something to you now that I've never, ever said before to anyone.'

She looked worried.

He smiled. 'Hey, it's not that bad. Just that I love you.'

Her eyes narrowed. 'You didn't say that in London.'

'Would you have believed me?'

'Probably not,' she admitted.

'I love you, Amanda.' He paused. 'Will you marry me?'

If he'd said that to her in London…

But he hadn't.

He was only saying it now because she'd just told him she was pregnant. He didn't really want *her*. Just like her parents hadn't really wanted her.

'No.' The word was dragged from her. No. She couldn't marry someone who didn't want her. Couldn't chain herself to spending the rest of her life in the country, so far away from the world she'd worked so hard for, with someone who didn't really want her. Been there, done that, never again. Last time, she hadn't had a choice. This time, she did. And she wasn't going to do it.

'What do you mean, no?'

'I'm not going to marry you.'

He frowned. 'Why not?'

Did he really need it spelled out? 'This is the twenty-first century. You don't need to get married just because you're having a baby.'

'Ah.' He stroked her cheek and gave her the sweetest, sweetest smile she'd ever seen. 'You think I'm only asking you because of the baby.'

Her throat felt as if it were clogged with sand. Just as well, because otherwise she'd be crying an ocean. 'Well, aren't you?'

'No.'

He expected her to believe that?

As if she'd asked the question aloud, he said softly, 'I was in a relationship a few months back. Nina wanted to get serious; I didn't. When I tried to end it, things got messy. I ended up having to get my solicitor to send her a letter. It sorted things out, but I decided then I wasn't going to get burned like that again. I had a life I liked: my home, my dog, my family, my job. I thought I was fine. Keep all my relationships strictly for fun.' He paused. 'And then Miss Wrong walked into my life.'

'Miss Wrong.' That was exactly what he thought of her. She tried to wriggle off his lap, but he wouldn't let her; he kept his arms very firmly round her.

'Or so I thought when I met her. Miss Wrong. My complete opposite. Everything I thought I didn't want—someone from my parents' world, someone who was undomesticated and lived on junk food and wouldn't know a rare plant from a weed. Someone who was neat and tidy and bossed me about. I should've wanted to drop her in the Cam and send her back to London. Except there was something about her. Something that made me feel…different. Protective, even.'

What? That was utterly ridiculous. She could look after—

'Which was crazy,' he continued, as if reading her thoughts, 'because I knew she was more than capable of looking after herself. She's the most capable woman I've ever met. Clever and competent and…' he took her hand and pressed a kiss into her palm, then folded her fingers over it '…so damned sexy I could barely keep my hands off her. With my head, I knew it was completely wrong. But I couldn't help myself. I wanted her so badly.'

It had been the same for her. Unexpected, unwanted…and irresistible.

'Lust,' she said, striving to sound cool and collected.

'It wasn't lust,' he said, his voice utterly sincere. 'It was more than that. A lot more. She made me feel *whole*. Because her differences fill the empty spaces in me, just as my differences fill her empty spaces. I can cook; she can't. She's organised; I'm untidy. Apart, we both have something missing. Together…' He stroked her face tenderly. 'Together, we make a fabulous team.'

She remembered the last time he'd said that to her. The night they'd made love. *It's not a competition. It's teamwork.*

'And now we're going to make an even better team,' he said. 'You, me and our baby. Our family.' He brushed his mouth very lightly against hers. 'I love you, Amanda. My world's a better place with you in it. So how about it?'

She still couldn't say yes. Because it wasn't just him to think about, was it? 'Will, I'm not going to fit in. Your sister doesn't like me.'

'You're not marrying Fliss, you're marrying *me*. And I think, once she actually gets to know you, she'll change her mind about you.'

How could he be so sure, when she wasn't? 'What about the rest of your family?'

He smiled. 'Helen and Martin sent you here. Doesn't that tell you anything?'

She thought about it for a moment. They wouldn't have told her where he lived if they'd disliked her on sight. Or if they thought he hadn't missed her. 'Oh.'

'Oh,' he mimicked, rubbing his nose against hers. 'Amanda, it's going to be fine. We'll have a new life. A better life. The best bits of yours and the best bits of mine. Teamwork. I want to marry you. Because you're *you*,' he emphasised, 'not because you're pregnant.'

How she wanted to believe him. But she couldn't. 'I…need time to think.'

He looked at her. 'Okay. You didn't drink your coffee. It's cold. I'll get you another one.'

'Will—thanks, but no. I can't face coffee right now,' she admitted.

'Then I'll get you something cold. Come into my kitchen.' He eased her to her feet, stood up, took her hand and led her through to the kitchen.

Wow.

Double wow.

Instead of the tiny little galley-style kitchen Amanda had expected, the room opened out into a high-ceilinged conservatory, and from there into the garden. Entranced, she let go of Will's hand and walked into the conservatory and looked out at the garden. There was an old-fashioned apple tree at the bottom, and a greenhouse and a vegetable patch—all looking incredibly neat and tidy. Next to the garden room was a shady patio with pots of bright red geraniums and herbs, and a table and chairs.

'I eat outside when I can,' he told her, handing her a glass of cold water with ice and a slice of lime.

Ha. Trust Will to go for the foodie option. Lime rather than lemon.

'It's gorgeous.' And he'd said he'd move to London. For her. He'd give all this up for her.

How could he bear to do it?

As if he knew what she was thinking, he said, 'It's just a house and a garden. We can make another one. All it takes is a bit of time and patience.'

'You'd really give this up and move to London for me?' she asked.

He smiled. 'In a heartbeat. Without you, this is all monochrome. Scentless, tasteless, no birdsong.'

He meant it. He really meant it. His eyes were green and clear with sincerity

And as she looked out at the garden, she realised what she wanted. A little girl, running around this garden with the dog. A little boy planting sunflowers with his daddy. Herself—complete with MBA—coming home from the office in Cambridge.

Home.

To Will.

Here.

Because this was where she belonged. Punting on the Cam on a Sunday afternoon and wandering hand in hand with her man through Grantchester Meadows. Making snowmen in the garden with their children in winter. And partner in a big accountancy firm. She could have it all. With Will.

'Teamwork.'

'Hmm?' He looked quizzically at her.

She repeated his words back at him. 'The best bits of your life and the best bits of mine.' She smiled. 'Don't give up the house, Will. It's perfect.'

'So are you saying…?' Hope bloomed in his face.

And then she knew he really meant it. He really wanted her.

'Is the offer still open? Of moving in with you?'

He smiled back. 'Yes, but there's a condition attached.'

'What condition?'

'Most people would call it a wedding ring.'

'You're supposed to go down on one knee and ask properly.'

'I already did.'

'Not on one knee.'

'Trying to organise me again?' he teased.

Her smile broadened. 'Better get used to it.'

'Oh, I can get used to it. As long as it's *wifely* nagging.'

She coughed. 'One knee, Will.'

He rolled his eyes. 'You'd better say yes this time.'

'One knee.'

He dropped to one knee and took her hand. 'Amanda Neave, I love you. Will you do me the honour of being my wife?'

'William Daynes…' Words she'd never thought she'd say. Words that almost hurt because they came from so deep inside her. And although it scared the hell of out her, she knew that Will was going to be worth all the risks. He'd hold her hand and never let her fall. Make their life a rose garden—and keep her safe from the thorns.

'I love you too.'

His hand tightened round hers, as if he knew how much that admission had cost her. And his voice was slightly cracked as he asked, 'Yes or no?'

She couldn't resist teasing him a little. 'I thought gardeners were supposed to be patient?'

'Ah, now, if we're playing dirty…' He sucked the tip of her index finger into his mouth, and desire sparkled through her.

'Uh. That's cheating.'

'Yeah. And I shouldn't have done that because I think I'm more uncomfortable than you are, right now,' he admitted ruefully.

Lord, his mouth was so sexy. And she wanted to feel it against hers, right now. Wanted to feel it all over her body. She shook her hand free, dropped to her knees, and cupped his face. Her big, bad pirate. The man with hands gentle enough to protect the most delicate flower.

All hers.

She brushed her mouth over his. 'Then I guess I'll have to do something about that.'

He groaned. 'You're killing me. Amanda, you're the love of my life. I'm going to go crazy if I don't get an answer. Will you marry me, be my wife and my lover and the one I want to be with for the rest of our days? Yes or no?'

She smiled. 'Yes.'

EPILOGUE

Just over two years later

'MUMMY!' THE little girl ran straight to Amanda, missed her footing and fell.

Before she hit the kitchen floor, Will scooped her up and handed her to her mother. Amanda wrapped her arms around her daughter and spun her round. 'Hello, darling. My beautiful girl.' Her little girl, with Will's unruly hair, her own blue eyes and the sweetest, sweetest smile.

'Boo-ful,' Lily said as Amanda set her down on her feet, and blew a kiss.

Will smiled at her. 'You, Mrs Daynes, have got post.'

She kissed him lingeringly as she took the envelope from him. 'Mmm.' Then she glanced at the franking. 'Ah. Results.'

'Want me to open it?' Will asked.

'No.' She took a deep breath. 'Well, if I bombed out, I can always resit.'

He grinned. 'No chance. You'll have passed with flying colours.'

She opened it and scanned the page. 'Oh.' She shrugged, and folded the paper again.

Will stared at her in shock. 'You're *kidding*. No way in hell could my genius wife have failed an exam.'

She handed the letter to Will, who unfolded it again, read it, whooped and spun her round. 'Fantastic. I knew you'd do it!'

'Mummy dance,' said Lily. 'Lily dance. Sunny dance.'

Amanda laughed, picked up her daughter and spun her round, while the spaniel bounced round them in a circle with one of Lily's shoes in her mouth. 'You know, Will, things come in threes.'

'Uh-huh?' Will was delving in the fridge for a bottle of champagne.

'I wouldn't open that *just* yet,' Amanda said.

'So what's the other news?'

'Patrick called me in to the office today.' She beamed at him. She loved the office in Cambridge. So different from London... Or maybe it was different because Will was in her life. She'd become audit manager virtually as soon as she'd transferred to the Cambridge branch—and she'd fitted in with the team right from the start.

'And?'

'Guess who the new head of department is, as of next Monday morning?'

Will whooped again. 'MBA and promotion on the same day? Forget champagne. We're having dinner out tonight.'

'Pizza,' Lily said gleefully.

Will groaned and ruffled her hair. 'You've inherited your mother's junk-food tendencies, young lady.'

'Ah, but her dad's a foodie, so it'll be posh pizza,' Amanda said with a grin. 'I take it you haven't done your filing today?'

Will rubbed a hand over his face. 'Been busy painting with Lily,' he muttered.

She could see that. There were bits of paper with blobs of paint on them all over the kitchen and the garden room. A painting set that Lily's godmother Dee—who was having a ball in her new job as a television producer—had brought down the previous weekend.

'It's my day off, Mands,' he protested, seeing her expression. 'I'm not doing any filing on my day off.'

'I think you should,' Amanda said. 'There might be something you need to look at in your in-tray.'

'I doubt it.'

'There really might be something you need to look at,' she repeated.

Will rolled his eyes. 'Oh, for goodness' sake. It can wait.'

'No, it can't.'

'Your mummy,' he told Lily, 'is a control freak.'

'Troll feek,' Lily repeated dutifully, and beamed at her mother.

Amanda laughed and rubbed the tip of her nose against Lily's. 'You'll pay for that later, Will. When I teach her to bat her eyelashes and give a gorgeous smile so Daddy buys her really, *really* expensive shoes.'

'Yeah, yeah,' Will retorted, but disappeared into his study.

Amanda set Lily back on her feet, folded her arms, tipped her head on one side and counted.

She got to thirty-two before she heard his sharp intake of breath. And it took him less than five seconds to get back to her, waving the envelope that contained the test stick. 'Absolutely positive?'

She laughed. 'That's what two blue lines usually means.'

The last time she'd seen a test stick with those two lines, she thought her world had fallen apart. This time…this time, it was joy right from the start. Because she'd swapped the worst bits of her life for the best bits of Will's.

'Teamwork,' she said softly.

'Yeah.' He held her close. 'Together, we're unbeatable. You, me, Lily, Sunny—and our bump-to-be.'

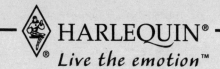

HARLEQUIN®
Live the emotion™

American **ROMANCE**®

Heart, Home & Happiness

HARLEQUIN® **Blaze**™

Red-hot reads.

HARLEQUIN®
E V E R L A S T I N G   L O V E™
Every great love has a story to tell™

 Harlequin® Historical
Historical Romantic Adventure!

HARLEQUIN®
H A R L E Q U I N   R O M A N C E®
From the Heart, For the Heart

HARLEQUIN®
INTRIGUE®
Breathtaking Romantic Suspense

Medical Romance™...
love is just a heartbeat away

**N**e**X**t™

*There's the life you planned.
And there's what comes next.*

**HARLEQUIN**®
Presents~
Seduction and Passion Guaranteed!

HARLEQUIN®
Super Romance®
Exciting, Emotional, Unexpected

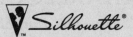

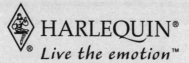

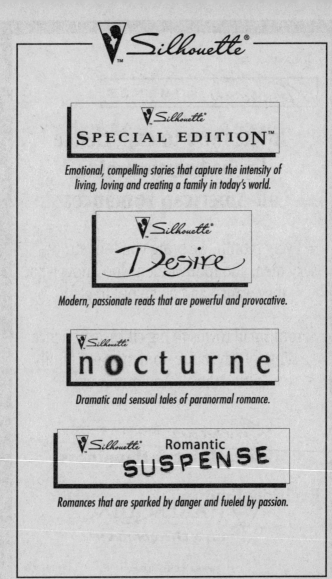

▼ *Silhouette*
SPECIAL EDITION™

Emotional, compelling stories that capture the intensity of living, loving and creating a family in today's world.

▼ *Silhouette*
Desire

Modern, passionate reads that are powerful and provocative.

▼ *Silhouette*
nocturne

Dramatic and sensual tales of paranormal romance.

▼ *Silhouette* Romantic
SUSPENSE

Romances that are sparked by danger and fueled by passion.

HARLEQUIN®

SuperRomance®

...there's more to the story!

Superromance.
A *big* satisfying read about unforgettable
characters. Each month we offer *six* very different
stories that range from family drama to adventure
and mystery, from highly emotional stories to
romantic comedies—and much more! Stories
about people you'll believe in and care about.
Stories too compelling to put down....

Our authors are among today's *best* romance
writers. You'll find familiar names and talented
newcomers. Many of them are award winners—
and you'll see why!

If you want the biggest and best
in romance fiction, you'll get it
from Superromance!

Exciting, Emotional, Unexpected...

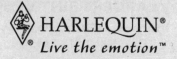

HARLEQUIN®
Live the emotion™

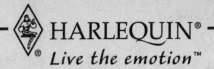